Everything

a *Songbird* novel

MELISSA PEARL

ISBN: 1511574968
ISBN-13: 978-1511574969

NOTE FROM THE AUTHOR

Singing has always been a part of who I am. I always have a song going through my head, and I can't count the number of times people will be talking and one little thing they say will make me think of a song. No matter where I am or what I'm doing, I feel like there is always a song for that moment.

I have absolutely adored writing Leo and Jody's story, and I've been able to live out some of my own dreams while writing theirs. I've always wanted to try my hand at composing a musical and during this story, I was able to compose three songs at my piano. I loved every second of it, and I'm tempted to keep going...to complete the work that Leo started. Who knows? Maybe one day I will.

The music in this book really matches the personality of the characters. Jody and Leo are both fun-loving, sunshine-type people, and I felt that sixties music was the perfect way to capture them. There are also a bunch of other favorites in here from musical numbers to current hits, but each song fits the moment. Many of the songs on this playlist are impossible for me not to sing along to. I hope you can get the same joy from listening and reading as I did from singing and writing.

EVERYTHING SOUNDTRACK

(Please note: The songs listed below are not always the original versions, but the ones I chose to listen to while constructing this book. The songs are listed in the order they appear.)

I DREAMED A DREAM

(From the musical Les Miserables)

Performed by Kerry Ellis

AS LONG AS YOU'RE MINE

(From the musical Wicked)

Performed by Idina Menzel & Leo Norbert Butz

THANK YOU FOR THE MUSIC

Performed by Amanda Seyfried

YOU'LL BE IN MY HEART

(From the Disney movie Tarzan)

Performed by Phil Collins

DREAM A LITTLE CRAZY

Performed by Architecture in Helsinki

ANGELIA

Performed by Richard Marx

YOU ARE MY SUNSHINE

Performed by Ray Charles

DREAM BIG

Performed by Ryan Shupe & The Rubberband

3 THINGS

Performed by Jason Mraz

I GOT YOU (I FEEL GOOD)

Performed by James Brown

DEFYING GRAVITY

Performed by Glee Cast

UGLY HEART

Performed by G.R.L.

GO

Performed by Boys Like Girls

HOW SWEET IT IS

Performed by Michael Buble

EMPIRE STATE OF MIND

Performed by Alicia Keys

MARRY ME

Performed by Jason Derulo

JESUS LOVES ME

Performed by James Morrison

DANCE WITH ME TONIGHT

Performed by Olly Murs

YAKETY YAK

Performed by The Coasters

YOU DRIVE ME CRAZY

Performed by Britney Spears

TITANIUM

Performed by David Guetta & Sia

MY GIRL

Performed by The Temptations

EVERYTHING

Performed by Michael Buble

LOVE

Performed by Cody Simpson & Ziggy Marley

SMILE

Performed by Sheppard

I WANT TO HOLD YOUR HAND

Performed by Sara Gordon

YOU MAKE ME HAPPY

Performed by Lindsey Ray

THE WAY YOU DO THE THINGS YOU DO

Performed by Gomez

YOU CAN'T ALWAYS GET WHAT YOU WANT

Performed by Glee Cast

NOTHING WITHOUT YOU

Performed by Olly Murs

BABY NOW THAT I'VE FOUND YOU

Performed by The Meanies

To enhance your reading experience, you can listen along to the playlist for EVERYTHING on Spotify.

https://open.spotify.com/user/12146962946/playlist/5d7paHBEYUHzRkVmwtEVvr

For Michael Buble -

Your smooth, honey voice and the way you've added a
fresh spin to classic songs from the past makes you a
total legend in my book.

ONE

JODY

The ivory keys were smooth beneath my fingers. I pressed middle C, repeating the action softly while I adjusted myself on the stool and looked up at the music in front of me. Tears burned my eyes as I played the first chord. The notes blurred on the page, but my fingers knew the song by heart, flying over the keys as the tune took shape. Pulling in a breath, I closed my eyes and started singing.

"I Dreamed A Dream" flowed from me in shaky waves, my voice crumbling on the long notes. I knew it was melodramatic. If Dad walked in right now and heard me singing this, saw the tears gliding down my cheeks, he'd probably roll his eyes, but after the night I'd just had, I felt justified in wallowing.

I was tired. I felt three times my age and I couldn't help lamenting the fact that this was not the plan! If things had gone the way I'd wanted, I'd have been six weeks into my sophomore year at The School of Theatre, Film and Television at the University of Arizona, no doubt working on my next solo piece, preparing to sing on stage, bathed in a spotlight.

I reached the chorus, my mind leaving the room and heading back to the last time I had stood on a stage, singing my very own solo.

I wasn't supposed to be in there, but I'd seen the back door ajar and couldn't resist taking a peek. I pulled the heavy curtain aside, a slow smile spreading over my lips as I padded across the stage and took my favorite spot — front and center. My mind's eye created a crowd in the darkened theatre. They sat anxiously awaiting my performance, and my body swelled with the euphoric buzz I lived for.

Pulling out my phone, I found the backing-track for "As Long As You're Mine" from the musical Wicked *and pressed play. The music sounded small and insignificant in the cavernous space, but my mind enhanced it to a full-blown orchestra. The melody moved through me, my body swaying to the beat as I surveyed the "crowd." Pulling in a breath, my lips drew into a smile as I started to sing.*

I imagined Stefan — I mean Mr. Kursato — sitting in

the audience, his intense gaze locked on me. Would he know each word out of my mouth was solely for him? The lyrics of this song had taken on a whole new level of sensuality since walking into his studio that first day. I meant every one of them.

I'd never made love before, but when I did, I wanted it to be with him. I know people always scoff at the idea of love at first sight, but it does happen.

It had happened to me.

My voice crescendoed over the line about him wanting me, and I pulled my hand toward my stomach, feeling the words as if they were my own. I closed my eyes and kept singing, my voice rising and falling as I practically begged my teacher to sleep with me.

I grinned at the very idea. It was insane. In spite of our undeniable connection, he would never see me as anything more than a student.

My voice trailed off as I sang the last line of the verse. The music picked up and I drew in a breath, ready to sing the male's side of the duet. But another voice filled the space. My eyes popped open and I spun to see Stefan—I mean Mr. Kursato—slowly walking across the stage toward me, his eyes dancing.

Holy hormones, he was hot. His fitted shirt was snug across his broad shoulders and covered his defined torso, which tapered down in that sexy triangle girls drool over. My roommate called him sex on a stick, so appropriate for Mr. K, but that's not what I'd fallen for. It was his chiseled face, that sharp, precise nose, that puff of perfectly styled hair that sat just right on his head...and those brown eyes. I nearly drowned in that chocolate gaze every time I was near him. And then there *was the way his lips moved as he sang...I wanted them on me.*

And his voice.

Oh, man, his voice! It was a perfect tenor, strong and clear. His lips rose into a half smile as he sang about falling under my spell, and with that look in his eye, I knew he meant it.

I thought I might die.

He reached me, his hand gently caressing my cheek as my part kicked in again. I sang the lines with him, our voices blending into a spine-tingling harmony I could feel in my core.

He wasn't acting.

Holy crap, he wasn't acting! He was singing these lines and meaning them!

My smile grew so wide I could barely form the words. We held the long notes together, his body so close I could feel it against me. I looked up at him and felt like a scared little kid, but hoped he'd read my shaky smile as sexy. The soundtrack petered off, and if we had been playing the roles of Elphie and Fiyero, we'd be whispering to each other, and then kissing.

Would he?

I held my breath, sweat prickling my palms as I lightly ran my hands up his toned arms. They rested on his rounded biceps as he gazed down at me, his eyes narrowing ever so slightly before softening with a look of wonder.

"You, singing on stage is...pure magic." His voice whistled right through me, sparking a passionate desire.

I opened my mouth to thank him, but he leaned toward me and all words were lost. The kiss started out as a light caress as if he was asking my permission. I leaned into it, applying a pressure that was hopefully inviting. He responded with a quick intake of breath, and then he was all-in, his hand cupping the back of my head and his tongue diving into my mouth as if this was our one and only time.

Maybe it was.

I didn't care.

I was going for it.

Nerves scuttled through my body, trying to distract me from the total euphoria of kissing the one and only man I'd ever been in love with.

"Jody," he panted.

I pressed my hips against his hard frame, feeling how much he wanted me.

Don't pull away, please!

Running my tongue along his bottom lip, I delved into the warm oasis of his mouth. He groaned in his throat and grabbed my hips, clutching the fabric of my loose summer dress until it strained against my butt.

"I want you."

"I want you, too," I whispered back, barely believing my luck. Was this some kind of dream?

"Ever since you walked into my studio, I haven't been able to stop thinking about this. Us. Together. If I don't pull away right now, I won't be able to stop myself...from having all of you."

I leaned back, gazing up at his gorgeous face and running my finger lightly down his chiseled jaw. "You can have all of me. I'm yours."

His lips pursed with indecision. I could see his small fight against temptation, and I was having none of it. I didn't care if I was his student, we wanted each other...we maybe even loved each other.

Curling my fingers around his neck, I skimmed my lips over his skin, lightly sucking his earlobe. A low moan reverberated in his chest. I looked up at him, my eyes wide, his filling with hunger.

"Are you sure?"

"I've wanted you since the second I laid eyes on you, so yeah, I'm one hundred percent sure."

His lips quirked with a smile, and he dove for my mouth again. My permission had fueled a new kind of fire in his veins, and his passion was both scintillating and startling. I met it head-on, not wanting to waste one second of this moment; it could be the only one I got.

Running his hands down my thighs, he scooped me up, his lips never leaving mine as he carried me backstage.

It was dark. The props and odd bits of furniture looked like black gargoyles in the silent space. Stefan smacked his shin on something and let out a soft curse. I giggled, wrapping my arms tighter around his neck as we toppled over and landed on a worn-out couch. His hands, set free from carrying me, roved my body, moving up my naked thigh and tugging at my underwear.

Whoa—he moved fast.

Too intoxicated with the moment, I arched my back, letting him pull my panties off, glad the shadows could hide my growing trepidation.

Would he know this was my first time?

Gently parting my legs, he settled between them, his tongue traveling down my neck as he squeezed one of my breasts.

"Jody, you feel amazing." His voice was hot and slick in my ear. I closed my eyes, running my hands beneath his shirt and marveling at the power of his back.

Could this really be happening?

He wanted me. My imagination over the last four weeks hadn't been on overdrive. Our unspoken desire had been real!

"Undo me," he whispered. At first I wasn't sure what he meant, but I soon figured out he was talking about his pants. I scrambled for his belt and buckle, my shaking fingers making the simple task a challenge.

As soon as his pants were loose, he helped me shimmy them down his hips, and then his weight was on me again.

I wasn't exactly sure what I was supposed to do, so I kept myself busy kissing his neck and face, hoping he wouldn't notice my complete ignorance.

He shuffled between me, gently moving my leg, and then I felt him pushing into me. I held my breath, clutching the back of his shirt and biting my bottom lip as a burning pain tore through my center. My eyes popped open, and I hampered the cry driving up my throat.

Stefan moaned in ecstasy, gliding his tongue up my neck before finding a rhythm. My body was so tense, I could barely move, but his soft hands coaxed me along and near the end, before he sank into me with a satisfied sigh, it almost felt good.

After catching his breath, he pressed his elbows into the couch, taking his weight off me and gently brushing a curl behind my ear.

"Was that—?"

"Hey! Who's in here? This is a restricted area, you know!"

Stefan jumped off me, yanking up his pants and scrambling to fasten them. He grabbed my panties off the floor, kissing them and giving me a cheeky wink before throwing them at me.

"Let's go," he whispered, tugging me into a run.

The flashlight searching the building swept across the stage. Stefan stilled and we could both see it was moving in our direction.

"Go this way." He turned me to the left and pushed me toward the door I'd snuck through. "I'll distract him. We can't get caught together."

I nodded mutely, still in a mild state of shock.

He planted a firm but fleeting kiss on my lips before brushing the tip of my nose with his thumb and smiling. "Go."

Before I could say more, he'd fled. The beam of light tracked my way, jolting me out of my stupor and making me rush for the door. I hit the night air and turned toward my dorm. Clutching my underwear in a fist, I wrapped my arms around myself and felt a warm trickle easing down my inner thigh.

For some reason, I wanted to burst into tears.

A feeble wail from the second floor made me flinch. Swiping the tears off my face, I stood and trudged up the stairs.

I'd lied to my family, told them his name was Stefan and he was my dance teacher. I mean, it *was* Stefan and he *was* a teacher, but he didn't teach dance and his official working title was Mario Kursato. His middle name was Stefan; he liked it better and let his students call him by that name behind closed doors.

In retrospect, I should have kept the teacher part to myself, but I figured a half-truth might be easier to go with.

I don't even know why I was trying to protect him. When I'd first mentioned to my sister, Morgan, how gorgeous he was, she knew nothing about him, so I guided her toward the idea of dance, a totally separate department, and kept my passion for my singing teacher completely hidden, even before he gave into temptation and bedded one of his students.

It was just easier. At least I thought it was. Every time I said dance class, I actually meant singing, and it seemed to work somehow...until the day I couldn't hide anymore.

TWO

JODY

I paused outside Angel's door, resting my head against the dark wood and preparing myself for a fussy afternoon. I couldn't blame her, really. My little six-month-old was teething and absolutely miserable, which in turn made me absolutely miserable. I felt like I'd tried everything over the past week, but nothing really comforted her. It was just something she had to live through. I understood that feeling all too well.

A fresh wave of tears formed as my fingers wrapped around the doorknob. I turned twenty last month; I shouldn't have to open the door to a crying daughter. Looking at my watch, I cringed. This time last year, I would have been opening the door to a small music studio which housed recording equipment, a baby grand, a bright green couch...and the man I was never supposed to love.

"Hey." Stefan's smile was soft as he greeted me.

I blushed, shutting the door behind me and tucking a large blonde curl behind my ear. I leaned against the door, gazing at him. It'd been three days since we'd done it backstage, and it was the first time I'd seen him since then.

He placed the sheet music he was holding onto the stand and approached me, his eyes flickering to the upturned blinds on the outer window. He'd always been a private person, didn't like prying eyes during lessons. I'd liked it, too. It meant I could give him my "I love you" eyes the whole lesson and no one else would know.

"How are you?" His voice was husky.

Mine shook. "I'm good."

"I wanted to call and check on you, but I couldn't dial your number, because I...shouldn't."

My gut clenched. Here it came, the "it was a mistake" speech. I clenched my jaw and kept my eyes averted, but he wouldn't let me look away.

Gently taking my chin, he turned me to face him. His head tipped to the side, his chocolate eyes filling with a tenderness I'd never seen before. Running his index finger softly down my cheek, he pressed his thumb against my lower lip and whispered, "Why didn't you tell me you were a virgin?"

I shrugged. "I don't know. I didn't want to hamper

the moment, I guess."

"You let me...be your first." He swallowed, his lips tipping into a soft smile.

"Because I love you." It was liberating to utter the words, even though I knew they could have him running for the hills.

But they didn't.

They made him grin.

"If I'd known..." He shook his head.

"What difference would it have made?"

His smile grew as he brushed the hair off my shoulder and lightly kissed my neck. "I would have taken it slow, forced myself not to get lost in the frenzied passion you stir within me."

Was he seriously saying this stuff to me?

I made him frenzied with passion?

Holy heckles! My grin was instantaneous.

"I would have delicately kissed every inch of your body," he murmured against my skin, melting my insides and sending my heart on a sprinting race. "I would have taken my time and shown you how amazing it can be."

"It was amazing," I lied, clutching his shoulders.

"It can be better." He reached behind me and locked the door before leaning back with a sparkling smile. "Let me show you." With a little wink, he turned and pressed play on his stereo. My voice filled the room, playing last week's recording of "Thank You For The Music."

I giggled, but the sound was swept away by a hot kiss.

With slow, tender hands, Stefan undressed me, his lips never leaving my skin. He stroked and teased me until my first real orgasm bloomed through my body, rocketing down my legs and making my eyes snap open. I gasped, the pleasure racing through me highly addictive.

I squeezed the back of his neck, arching my hips toward him. "I need you inside me now."

He chuckled, pausing to pull out a condom. Ripping it open, he rolled it on and gave me a sheepish smile. "Better safe than sorry, right?"

If he'd known it was already too late, he probably never would have touched me that day or any other singing lesson after that.

Angel's cries increased with fervor. I pushed open the door, putting on my happy face and pretending the memories didn't rock me.

I leaned against the bars of her crib and gazed down at her. Her tiny arms and legs were flailing and her cheeks were bright red...but damn, she was the cutest thing on the planet. In spite of my angst and growing animosity toward my lifestyle, I couldn't trade my little girl for anything.

"Hello, my angel." I smiled down at her.

Her pitiful wail paused momentarily as she looked at my face, her bright blue eyes taking me in before she opened her mouth and cried even harder.

"Okay, okay." I picked her up, lavishing her weight in my arms as I pressed her against me. I breathed in her sweet scent and reminded myself why I'd kept her. Kissing the blonde down on the top of her head, I held her close and hummed

"You'll Be In My Heart" from Tarzan. It was our song, and I meant each word as my humming changed to lyrics. Angel nuzzled into my neck, rubbing her wet cheeks against my skin, and all I could cling to was the hope that one day I'd stop wishing for things that would never come true, and pining for the man who had broken my heart.

THREE

LEO

I broke her heart. I was willing to take full blame for that. I never should have asked Gerry to marry me. I never should have promised her something I couldn't give.

"Mr. Sinclair, if you could please sign here and here, and at the bottom of the next page, as well." The lawyer's voice was quiet yet matter-of-fact.

I understood his need to keep emotion out of the proceedings. I wished I could do the same.

My throat was so clogged I could barely breathe.

My mother was going to hate me for the rest of eternity.

"How can you just give in, Leo? Marriage isn't supposed to be easy. You make it work!"

I flicked a quick glance at Gerry. Her glossy nails tapped on the wood as she watched me, her nervous little tic that I used to find adorable. I cleared my throat and squeezed the pen between my fingers, scribbling my name where I was supposed to and sliding the divorce papers across the table.

She gave me a short, tight smile as I handed her the pen and then signed her name next to mine.

She'd swept me off my feet when we first meet. The older woman. Haha—only by a few years, but my mates sure hassled me about it. Her stunning sophistication, her confidence. She felt so out of my league. All the guys had been drawn to her, but she'd chosen me. We got on great at first and everyone kept telling me what a perfect match we were.

"You and Gerry, aye?" My brother would nudge me with his elbow. *"Nice, mate."*

"You two are so gorgeous together," my mother would swoon. *"What kind of ring are you going to buy her?"*

"So when do you think you'll pop the question?" my boss would ask.

"Go for an outdoor wedding, mate, you won't regret it." Dad would wink at Mum.

They all chipped away at me, pressuring me from all sides until the golden boy caved and asked his first serious girlfriend for her hand. It had been magical, euphoric—

"Done." Gerry laid the pen on top of the papers and looked at me.

It was over.

She was no longer Mrs. Geraldine Sinclair.

"I'll get these papers finalized as soon as possible. It should only take a few days. Thank you for both being so amicable. It has made the division of assets so much easier."

We both nodded, both gave him strained smiles, our expressions nearly identical. Thank the Lord we hadn't owned property together...or had kids! I cringed just thinking about how much worse this could have been.

"If you have any questions, please give me a call." The lawyer nodded at us both.

With that, we thanked him and stood from our seats. I held the door for Gerry, and we walked to the lift in silence. Sliding my hands into my pockets, I waited in the awkward quietness, wondering if Gerry would ever talk to me again.

We'd been separated for twelve months and ten days. Australian law required that we had to be separated for a year before we could get a divorce. As soon as the anniversary loomed large, Gerry started the proceedings so we could fast-track it through and have the divorce finalized as soon as possible.

She never really told me why she was in such a hurry, but I went with it. I'd totally failed her; I was happy to go along with whatever she wanted.

The lift doors dinged open and we stepped inside.

"I'm getting married." Her voice was soft when she pressed the button for the ground floor, but I felt like she'd just hollered the words at me.

I pressed my lips together, holding in my initial shock.

With a slow swallow, I squinted at the muted metal in front of me and nodded. "Wow, ah, congratulations. Who's the lucky guy?"

"Brent Hancock."

"Brent!" Shit, I knew that guy. We'd been in youth group together. My eyebrows rose of their own accord. "You didn't waste your time, did ya?" I mumbled.

"Excuse me?" She whipped around to face me.

I cleared my throat, my brows bunching together as I tried to avoid eye contact.

"You left our marriage long before you walked out that door, Leo."

"Yeah, yeah, fair enough." I didn't want to get into an argument. She was right. I'd started pulling away before the honeymoon was even over.

We'd tried to make it work. It was an honest effort, but how did you make something work that was never meant to be in the first place?

Gerry would turn thirty next month. She'd wasted one year of her life dating me, two married to me and one getting over me. She had every right to move on and start the family she was craving...the family I refused to give her.

The lift doors opened, and we stepped out into

the glass-walled entranceway.

"When it's right, you just know it. There's no hesitation, it's easy." Gerry gave me a soft smile. "That's how it is for me and Brent. I have no reservations at all about marrying him."

Unlike me. I could hear her unspoken words. Both of us went into our marriage with blinders on, but deep down, we knew.

I nodded. "Brent's a top guy. I'm happy for you, Gerry."

"Really?" Her dry voice and arching eyebrows made me grin.

"I'm serious. You deserve it." I patted her shoulder. "I want you to find your happy, and if Brent can do that for you, then...great." I forced a smile.

Her expression crumpled with sympathy. "Oh, Leo." She rose toward me and kissed my cheek. "You're like a little lost soul." She rested her hand on my face, running her nails lightly through my stubble. "I hope you find your way. I hope you..." She dropped her hand with a sigh. "I hope you can figure out what it is you really need."

FOUR

JODY

"Okay, what else do I need?" I mumbled the words as my eyes scanned down the list.

Angel replied with a small burp that made me grin.

"Thanks for your help."

She gave me a gummy smile, a long string of drool hanging off her lower lip. I wrinkled my nose and swiped it away with my finger, quickly rubbing it on my jeans.

So gross! Never thought I'd be okay with that, but parenthood changes things.

I paused the shopping cart next to the shelves of

diapers and hunted out the cheapest, yet not completely useless, brand Morgan had discovered a couple of weeks ago. My older sister was so much better at shopping than I was. If I could have my way, I'd buy the best of everything, screw the money, but she made me stop and think all the time.

"Where do you think this money comes from, Jody? You can't spend whatever you want. We made a budget for a reason!"

I rolled my eyes. I'd been forced to give in, because I was the only member of the household not actually earning anything. I cringed just thinking about it, but there was no way I was putting Angel into daycare while I went and worked at a grocery store. Once again, Morgan worked the numbers, and we figured out I'd be spending eighty percent of my income on childcare. Since I wasn't qualified for anything, I really had no other option but stay-at-home mom, which I was okay with...most days.

I rubbed the fluff on Angel's head as she kicked her legs. With a little squeal, she demanded I get moving. I found the diapers and threw them in. The song on the radio caught my ear, and I grinned at my daughter.

"This is your song, cupcake." I joined in with Richard Marx, singing "Angelia" with him while Angel watched me wide-eyed, kicking her legs again before getting bored and chomping down on her plastic teether.

The song was lifting my spirits as I wove the

shopping cart into the next aisle, but my high was stolen by two girls who looked to be my age.

They stood in front of the condoms, giggling over which packet to buy.

"I can't believe it's happening tonight." one of them squealed.

"Ray is so freaking hot. You're so incredibly lucky!"

"He'll be my perfect first time." Her cheeks flushed pink.

I wanted to plant my hand on my hip and say, *Really? Are you sure about this guy? Are you sure you love him? Because it should be a mutual thing, you know. If you don't think he feels the same way, cross your legs, honey, and walk away.*

She caught me staring at her, her eyes darting to Angel before catching mine again. I tried to stand tall against the silent judgment and noticed her reach for a second packet.

"Just to be safe," she muttered as she glided past me.

I tried to ignore their snickers. Angel was so obviously my daughter with her blue eyes and blonde fuzz, her little button nose that would grow to look just like mine. As handsome as Stefan was, I was kind of glad she didn't resemble him very much. At least every time I looked at her, I wasn't reminded of his rejection...well, almost every time.

"Jody, honey, what's wrong?" He sat me down on that green couch. The one we'd turned into a love bed almost every time I came in here, but not lately. I just

couldn't do it.

"You can't keep saying everything's fine. Your singing's off. You've lost your shine. We haven't slept together in nearly three weeks. You keep fobbing me off with excuses." He ran his hand gently up my arm. "I need the truth."

"I don't think you want to hear it."

He frowned, making his face look sharp and unfamiliar.

"Stefan, I'm pregnant."

His fingers left my arm in a flash; he practically fell off the couch as he lurched away from me. "Are you sure?"

"Yes."

"Well, how far? I mean when did this happen? We're always so careful."

"Not the first time."

His skin paled, making him look sick. He closed his eyes, running a hand through his light brown hair. "Shit. This can't be happening."

I swallowed, hating his reaction. "What are we going to do?"

"We?" He jerked to look at me.

My face crumpled with a frown. "Yes, we."

"Um, yeah, we, um...Jody, honey, I don't—I can't—This..." His chuckle was hollow and breathy. "I'm your teacher. I'm not supposed to be sleeping with you."

"But you did."

"Yeah." He nodded. "And it was wrong and we should probably stop."

My lips parted, my chest so tight I couldn't speak.

"I'm sorry," he whispered. "I can't get fired over this.

It could destroy my career, everything I'm working toward."

"But what am I supposed to do?"

He shrugged. "You could, you know, get rid of it." He winced. "Then when it's done, you could come back, and it would be like nothing has changed."

"Except you wouldn't want to sleep with me anymore." My voice was sharp.

He cringed, his face buckling as he shuffled back to my side. "Jody, that's not true. I've loved our time together."

"Just not me."

"What?"

"You don't love me."

"I do." He nodded, reaching for my hand.

I snatched it away before he could get a proper grasp. "No, you don't."

It took all my strength to stand from the couch and walk for the door.

"Jody, please."

I paused, my hand on the doorknob. When he didn't say anything, I slowly turned back to face him. I don't know what my blue gaze was doing, but guilt crested over Stefan's expression before he licked his lower lip and glanced at the floor.

"Just don't do anything rash. You need to think this through, Jody. Really consider all your options."

"What the hell do you think I've been doing!" I threw my hands wide.

"Have you told anyone?" His voice hitched. "I mean—"

"No." I cut him off before the ugly look of fear on his

face marred my memory of him. "Your secret's safe with me."

The relief washing over his face nearly killed me. I bolted from the room before my body broke down like it wanted to and I turned into a weeping puddle on the floor.

I didn't blame him. If I'd been in his position, I probably would have done the same thing...maybe. When the school found out I was pregnant and asked me to leave, I went rushing back to his office in tears, my last feeble attempt to appeal to his humanity. He'd held me close until I stopped crying, but he hadn't changed his mind. He hadn't dropped to his knee and proposed like I was dreaming he would, claiming me and my baby as his own.

With my tail between my legs and my heart in pieces, I'd fled back to LA, Morgan, and my irate father, while Stefan had gone on to do who knows what. Morgan and Dad were the only people who knew he was my teacher and even then, they still thought he'd taught me dance. I'd kept his secret safe this whole time, and I'm not even sure why.

I couldn't help wondering if he was bedding another student on that green couch of his. My gut clenched, the idea making my vision fuzzy.

His biggest mistake was sleeping with someone he wasn't in love with; mine was giving my heart to someone who didn't feel the same way.

He'd never once tried to contact me after that hideous day. He had no idea he was the father of a little girl named Angelia. She had no ties to him. I'd put *father unknown* on the birth certificate and given her my last name. If Angel needed to find out later, I'd tell her the truth, but the idea scared me senseless. I couldn't think of anything worse than telling her "Daddy" wanted nothing to do with her. How did I sell the story without making myself out to be a senseless slut? How was I supposed to encourage her to follow her dreams, and make her believe that anything could happen, when I'd torn mine up and thrown them to the wind?

I absentmindedly ran my fingers through her blonde fuzz.

Some days I couldn't believe I'd actually had the courage to keep her. If I'd given her up for adoption like my original plan, I'd be back in Tucson, Arizona, reaching for my star-studded future.

Angel dropped her teether.

I bent to collect it up, wiping it on my sweater and hoping the five-second rule applied in a grocery store. I pursed my lips as I hesitantly gave it back to her, but I knew she'd throw a complete fit if I took it away.

It went straight back in her mouth, drool coating it quickly.

My nose wrinkled again.

"Babies are gross." I stuck out my tongue.

She replied with a heart-stopping smile, her eyes dancing with adulation. I kissed her head and pushed the shopping cart forward. She was adorable, but she was also six months old and she would be depending on me for the rest of forever. That's what it felt like anyway.

I glanced over my shoulder as I left the aisle, spotting the row of condom packets. I couldn't imagine ever buying one of those again. I was a single mother; who would ever want me now?

FIVE

LEO

The water was still, out on the pond. Flies buzzed around our heads, reminding us that summer was looming and they'd soon be a bloody pain in the arse.

"Piss off," Kev grumbled, flicking his hand in front of his face, the standard Aussie wave.

"Come on, mate, they're just like flirting with ya." I grinned.

"Yeah, well, I'm gunna keep playing hard to get. I'm married, you little black beasts!" he yelled at the insects, making the boat rock.

"Whoa, calm down." I flung out my arms to

steady us, trying not to let go of my fishing rod in the process.

My older brother settled, apart from his foot that kept tapping.

"It's my time off, mate. I get harassed relentlessly at home by four of my own little beasts. I don't need the flies adding to it."

"Aw, come on, your kids are amazing."

"Uncles are supposed to say that." His voice was dry, but he was hampering a grin. He was a great dad...and was becoming a great farmer, too.

I had to razz him, though; it was a younger brother's duty.

"Farm life not suiting you, aye?"

He grinned. "It suits me just fine."

We both chuckled and then fell into our comfortable "fishing time" silence. I closed my eyes, soaking in the hot rays and breathing in the scent. Kev's little farm was more of a lifestyle block than anything. Having suffered a heart attack over a year ago, my big brother decided to change more than just his diet.

Getting a phone call that the guy I'd worshipped since before I could walk was being rushed to hospital in cardiac arrest had terrified me. It had rocked the whole family pretty bad. Kev was built like a brick shit-house, a bloody unshakeable force. A guy like him didn't have heart failure...and his wife, Deb, was determined he'd never have it again.

She'd made him quit his high-powered, *work a billion hours a week* job, and they'd moved an hour out of the Sydney suburbs. It must have cost a frickin' bomb, but they did it anyway...and it was doing them good. A few cows, goats, and a small flock of sheep—they were making it work.

"So, how'd it go the other day?" Kev looked over at me.

"Yeah, yeah, smooth as expected." I jiggled my line, hoping for a nibble. "She's getting married again."

"No shit?"

"Yeah, Brent Hancock. Remember him?"

"I remember his older sister." Kev gave me a sly smile.

I chuckled.

"They were a nice family, the Hancocks."

"Yep." I cut the word short.

"Mum must be going mental."

"Yeah, she's on the rampage at the moment."

"You know you've got to ignore her, right?"

"She makes it bloody hard."

"For you in particular." Kev slapped me on the shoulder. "You were her golden boy. She had your life mapped out for you the second you sat down at the piano, you little Mozart."

I sighed, knowing he was right. I'd acquiesced to all of it, so eager to please, desperate for her pride.

"You've got to get out, mate."

"I'm trying to. There's a little granny flat I might be able to rent near school."

"Mate, you need to move out of the bloody country to get away from her complaints."

"It's the circles she's in. People do not get divorced. I've embarrassed her."

"Who gives a shit! It's your life. You can do what the hell you want with it. You and Gerry were sucking each other dry."

My line sat dead in the water, feeling much like my insides.

"Leo, you're turning twenty-seven in two days. You're still living at home with two judgmental parents, miserable as hell. What's your plan?"

I scoffed. "I don't have one, Kev."

He cuffed me on the back of the head. I lurched in my seat and told him to F-off.

His chuckle wasn't hindered by my vicious glare but thankfully died down when I turned away from him.

"What do you want out of life, little brother?" he asked.

I shook my head.

"Come on, use your brain. You've always gone along with what everyone else wanted, but this is your chance. Nothing is holding you here. You can go and be whatever the hell you want."

I nibbled my bottom lip.

"If you could have any dream come true, what would it be?" Kev flicked me on the arm with his hand. "Come on, what?"

I cleared my throat and threw a quick glance at him, rubbing my finger under my nose.

"You'll think it's dumb."

"Tell me anyway."

"Well, you know that Christmas production I

did for church last year?"

"Yeah, yeah, that was awesome. The kids loved it."

"Me, too; more than I thought I would. I felt alive and passionate throughout that whole thing. I mean, I love teaching, don't get me wrong; it's a great gig. But writing music, directing the cast and seeing my stuff come together on a stage, that was..." I shook my head. "Pure magic."

"Then that's what you should do. Quit your job and become a composer."

"Mum would never forgive me. Did you see the look on her face when they offered me Director of Music at St. Regis College next year?"

"He'll be the youngest person to ever be in that position in the history of the school." Kev put on a voice, badly imitating my mother. "It's one of the most prestigious high schools in Sydney, you know." He ended with an eye-roll, his tongue dangling out of his mouth in disgust.

Mum used that damn line all the time.

My grin was lopsided and fleeting. "She stopped hating me for my failed marriage long enough to actually give me a smile, Kev. It's the first time she's properly spoken to me since I left Gerry."

"Would you forget about her, you whiny little mummy's boy."

I flipped him the bird.

Kev chuckled, lightly punching my arm before turning to me with a serious gaze. "Leo, tell me your ultimate dream, mate. Don't think about anyone but you, no restrictions, nothing. Just pretend I'm a genie and tell me what you'd wish for."

My grin was sheepish when I finally admitted, "Genie, I wish to see a Leo Sinclair musical on a Broadway stage."

My older brother went still for a minute, his eyes slowly lighting with a look of pride. His lips rose with a smile. "Then go and take it."

I threw him a cynical glance. "It's not like I can just ring up a producer and say 'hey, I'm talented, take my musical and then pour a shitload of money into it and help me bring it to life'."

"Why not?"

"Because, stuff like that doesn't happen."

"Not unless you try to make it happen."

I shrugged, digging my thumbnail into the padding of the fishing pole. "I get to direct the high school plays at St. Regis, that's good enough for now. I just wish I had more time to write my own stuff. Maybe if I worked my arse off over the summer break I could put something together and—"

"Oh, would you shut the fuck up." Kev shook his head. "You said Broadway, and I don't care how prestigious your bloody high school is, it's not what you ultimately want. Why settle?"

"Kev, how the hell am I supposed to get what I want?"

"Well, you could start by writing a musical and then I don't know, send them a demo."

"It's not that easy. You need connections, you

can't just send in your stuff."

"Well, you've got one, mate!"

My brow bunched tight as I turned to look at him.

"Uncle Bobby."

Our godfather and my dad's best friend from decades ago.

"You really think he'd help me?"

"Well, for a start, he's American and Broadway is *in* America."

"Yeah, I know where Broadway is."

"So, move your arse over there and start selling your songs."

"I don't know if Bobby can get me in."

"Aw, come on, mate. The guy takes his morning swims in greenbacks. He's got more connections than anyone else I know. He'll get you into the States, and he'll get your stuff in front of the right eyes."

A thrill raced through me as I let my imagination loose. It was like opening a trap door with rusty hinges, but as the idea crept out of the narrow space, a hopeful smile bloomed on my lips.

"Do you think I should?"

"Leo, do us all a favor and stop living the life everyone else wants you to. Chase your dreams. Even if they never come true, at least you tried, and that's got to count for something. Dreams are fuel for the soul. Don't be scared. Dream a little crazy." He shrugged. "It might come true."

I sang the first line of "Dream A Little Crazy" by the indie band Architecture in Helsinki.

Kev chuckled. "Always got a song for everything. That's our Leo." He patted me on the shoulder.

I shrugged, trying to hide the surge of emotion racing through me. Could I do it? Could I seriously step way out of my comfort zone and finally take charge of my own life?

The idea was so liberating I wanted to whoop a war cry.

"Broadway, here I come," I whispered under my breath, my lips stretching into the widest smile I think I'd ever made.

SIX

JODY

I wished I could just get away from it all and start over some days. I was so tired I actually felt numb. After seven long weeks, Angel's teeth had finally come through, four little biters that could do damage if you weren't fast enough. But now she had a cold...and the whole damn house knew about it.

She'd been up most of the night, which meant I'd been up most of the night, and I was taking the term *living dead* to a whole new level. I thumped down the stairs, desperate for some caffeine before Angel woke and I'd have to deal with her again. I wasn't wearing my watch, but I was guessing the time was somewhere around eight-ish? Damn, I must have only scored about three hours sleep the night before.

"Please nap well today, Angel," I mumbled as I stepped toward the kitchen.

"So, what did you say?" Dad's voice was tight and I immediately flinched, even though he wasn't talking to me. It'd been tight a lot lately, putting me on edge every time I was around him. I paused outside the kitchen, not wanting to reveal myself.

"No, of course." Morgan's reply was terse.

"You can't keep doing that. He'll stop asking."

My older sister sighed. "We love each other. We don't need to be married."

"Hey, stop lying to yourself. His filming schedule has just picked up again, hasn't it? Huh?"

There was a pause while I assumed Morgan nodded. I pressed my hand against the wall, forcing myself not to peek in for a look. The second they spotted me, this conversation would end and I wanted to know why they were bickering about Morgan's relationship with her super-hot boyfriend, Sean Jaxon.

"Do you know how I know?"

"Dad..."

"You've been grumpy. When Sean was on vacation over the Christmas break, you were bubbly and happy and no one could have wiped that smile off your face."

"I don't want to have this conversation."

"Tough luck, sugar. We're having it. You can't

keep doing this to yourself. You are dating a very busy actor. His filming schedule during the week is insane, and unless you move your butt in with him, you'll never get to see him."

"It works, Dad."

"For how long? How many proposals do you think he has in him? Why do you think he keeps asking?" Dad filled Morgan's silence with the answer everybody (and I literally mean that) already knew. "Sean Jaxon is in love with you and he wants to make a life with you. He wants you to live with him so he can see you for more than a few hours every Sunday!"

"I know that!" Morgan's voice shot into the air. "But how I am supposed to say yes right now! The timing's not exactly perfect."

"So, what, you're gonna wait until your niece is eighteen?"

I flinched. Angel? She wasn't saying yes to Sean because of Angel? That was insane!

"Jody needs me right now," Morgan mumbled.

"She'll be fine." Dad punched out the words.

"Oh, come on, *now* who's lying?"

I bit down hard on my lip, trying to avert the sting of her comment.

"You guys barely talk to each other. How would you function if I wasn't here? Who would look after everything? Who'd cook? Clean? Do the laundry?"

"We all pitch in."

"Only when I tell you to. I write the grocery list each week, I separate the colors and the whites, I make a weekly meal plan! I cook dinners you can freeze!" Tears burned as I listened to Morgan's voice rise. "That's how it works. You bring in the money, Jody looks after the baby, and I do everything else. And until that changes, I can't move out."

My ears rang with her words, my throat thickening into a tight tube that made it hard to swallow.

Dad's sigh was deep and heavy, reflecting the aching thump in my heart. "You've sacrificed so much to look after Jody and me. When's that going to stop? You can't give us the rest of your life. I don't want you losing out again. I can't imagine you getting over a guy like Sean." The way he mumbled the last line made me think of Mom...and the fact my dad had never really gotten over her, even after she walked out on us, forcing Morgan to become the mother of the family.

I bit my lip, hating that I understood that loyal stupidity.

Damn Stefan and those chocolate eyes of his.

"He's not going to break up with me, Dad. He understands. Family first, remember?"

"Sean is your family now, too."

I could picture Morgan fighting for the right words, probably throwing Dad a tight smile. "I have a late class at the dance studio tonight. Dinner is defrosting in the sink. All you guys have to do is heat it. Jody's probably not going to be up for much after her night with Angel, so don't get her to do the laundry or anything, I'll sort that out when I get home."

Dad humphed.

"I appreciate your concern, Dad. I love that you care so much about me."

I heard a rustling. Morgan was no doubt wrapping Dad in a hug.

I missed his hugs. He was like a big, cuddly bear, and he used to squeeze me extra tight, singing "You Are My Sunshine," the Ray Charles version...always the Ray Charles version. The grin brought on by my cherished memory quickly faded. He'd barely smiled at me since I'd moved back home, and he never called me 'sunshine' anymore.

"I just hate that you're in this position. One mistake and it's affecting all of us."

His words were like fists to my chest. I knew exactly which mistake he was referring to, one he refused to actually talk to me about. No, instead he burned the errors of my ways into me with his disappointed gazes and frowning lips, his heaving sighs and muttered greetings. His little superstar, set for Broadway, got knocked up by her teacher and screwed up everything...and he was never going to let me forget it.

I sniffed at my tears, lurching for the stairwell. Screw the coffee. I just needed to get the hell out of the house.

Angel roused as I walked into the room and she started crying immediately. I pulled out her warm hoodie and thick socks, gently putting them on her before strapping on my front pack and nestling her inside. Grabbing the diaper bag off the floor, I checked that my wallet was inside before throwing a soft blanket over my baby and walking for the door.

"Come on, Angel, let's get out of here."

SEVEN

LEO

"Dream Big" by Ryan Shupe and The Rubberband was blasting in my ears as I trotted down the stairs and out onto the street. It was my new anthem, and I'd lost count of how many times I'd listened to it over the last couple of months. Since my chat with Kev, I'd thrown caution to the wind and jumped after my dreams. My mother hadn't spoken to me since I refused the Director of Music offer and bought a ticket to the States. It was surprisingly liberating, and although I'd love to patch things up with her at some stage, I certainly wasn't missing her. Dad kept me updated in his weekly emails. By the sounds of it, now that her golden boy was gone she was throwing all her pressure and attention onto her baby girl. It hadn't taken my sister much to forgive me. If anything, I think she was lavishing the attention.

"She can have it." I chuckled under my breath.

Before heading down the street, I turned and looked up at the building Bobby had put me in charge of. It had been his way of getting me a work visa. I was now employed by my godfather as the property manager of a six-story apartment building five blocks back from the Santa Monica Pier. Apparently, I was the only man for the job. I grinned as I thought about how good Bobby had been to me. He'd pulled all the right strings to secure me this chance, and I wasn't about to waste it.

Sure, LA wasn't New York or Broadway, but it was a heck of a lot closer than Sydney, Australia, and Bobby was already working on speaking with the right people. I was hoping to get a musical finished by the middle of the year so I had something decent to present. I'd had a few ideas, but nothing solid. A million melodies lived in my head, fighting for first place, but the lyrics were still amiss. What I needed was a theme...or at least a spark of inspiration that would set me on track.

Taking a left, I loped down the street and enjoyed the sunshine. The air was crisp, but with a sky so blue, you couldn't really complain. I tapped the paper I was holding lightly against my other hand as I walked, wondering if my plan would actually work. I'd checked with Bobby and he'd okayed it, as long as it didn't affect the running of his building.

I was pleased with how quickly I'd managed to settle in. I'd introduced myself to the tenants and assured them that I would take good care of them as long as they paid me their rent on time. Things were running smoothly. I knew I'd have to keep an eye on a few of them, and Ms. Thornby was going to be pretty bloody demanding, but I could handle her. I grinned as a song fired through my head. Yes, it was the perfect choice for that woman.

Rounding the next corner, I spotted the community bulletin board I was aiming for. I'd decided to start there. It was free to pin up my notice, and if I got no bites, I'd pay for local paper advertising next week.

I spotted a young woman standing beside the board. Her long waves of golden hair were the first thing to catch my attention, and the fact she kept wiping her face as she gazed at the various bits of paper, haphazardly attached with pins and staples. It wasn't until I got closer that I realized she was crying. She must have spotted me out of the corner of her eye because she stiffened, a protective hand cradling the blanket-wrapped bundle attached to her front.

Shit, I hoped she was a nanny. She was way too young to be a mother. Although, she could be one of those lucky people who looked young for their age or something.

I didn't say anything as I stepped behind her

and searched for the best place to pin my ad.

She sniffed, her breath a little hiccupy—she must have been crying pretty hard. Her delicate hands rubbed the bundle's back. I assumed her baby was sleeping because she was doing that swaying thing my sister-in-law did when her kids were young. Back and forth, back and forth.

Yeah, this blonde chick was a mum all right. Crikey, she was young.

I couldn't help wondering what her story was.

She was pretty, that's for sure. That cute little pointy nose and those round blue-green eyes, combined with the luscious locks of hair made her a real stunner.

I found a good spot on the board and pulled a pin from my pocket, jabbing it through my bright blue piece of paper. Her eyes darted to it, but when she noticed me look at her they flicked back to the other side of the board. Another tear ran down the side of her cheek. She didn't bother to wipe it away.

I knew it was time for me to go, but I felt awful leaving. Her tears would tug at any guy's heart. Pulling in my breath, I held it for a beat then turned to her, taking the bud out of my ear so she could see I wanted to chat.

"I don't mean to intrude, but are you okay?"

My Aussie accent took her by surprise. I could tell by the way her eyes rounded. She got over it quickly and pulled her expression into line, giving me a small, tight smile instead.

"I'm just having a bad day," she murmured.

"I'm sorry."

She shrugged, slashing the latest tear off her cheek and sniffing again.

"Do you like music?"

Again, I took her by surprise. She looked straight at me then, nearly knocked me clean off my feet with that gaze of hers. Geez, her eyes were beautiful.

I glanced at the notice board to kill the connection but turned back when she said, "Yeah, I love music."

I grinned. "Me, too. If you can find the right song for the moment, it can make everything better."

She nodded, her smile growing slightly, although she obviously wasn't convinced. I bet she was thinking nothing could possibly make this moment better for her.

Time to prove her wrong.

I had to admit, I did feel awkward having this conversation with a total stranger, but I decided that I didn't care what she thought. I'd been trying to live up to other people's expectations my whole life and look where it had gotten me.

It was time for me to start being unhindered, unhampered Leo, and this crying girl next to me was as good a place as any to start.

"There's this great song by Jason Mraz called '3 Things.' Do you know it?"

"I know Jason Mraz, but I don't know if I've heard that one yet."

"Well, it's a good one. I always listen to it when

I'm having a crapper of a day."

She bit her lips together, obviously fighting a smile.

I didn't know what I'd said that was so funny, but I powered on. "It somehow has this magical quality, and it always makes me feel better."

"'3 Things' by Jason Mraz." She nodded. "I'll look it up."

"Alrighty then." I grinned, feeling proud of myself for following my instinct and talking to her. "I hope your day gets better."

"Thanks." Her voice was soft, her smile sweet.

I nodded a silent farewell and put the bud back in my ear, tugging the phone out of my back pocket and finding an upbeat song to walk home to.

I couldn't help a glance over my shoulder as I walked away, and a smile took over my face. She had her earplugs in and was searching for something on her phone.

Man, I hoped my suggestion worked.

EIGHT

JODY

I pulled out my phone as soon as the guy with the weird accent walked away. Spotify was already open, and I did a quick search on Jason Mraz. "3 Things" was on his *YES!* album, which I hadn't had a chance to listen to yet. Pressing the title, I waited for my 3G to spin, and then Jason's voice filled my head.

I stood stock-still listening to the words as if my life depended on it. My eyes grew wide as he talked about his life falling apart and how he'd cry whenever that happened. I looked up the road and watched the guy lope away.

A smile eased over my face as Jason kept singing. The music picked up with a merry tune that seemed out of place, but then the second verse kicked in. I closed my eyes and breathed in through my nose. I felt my chest expand, the cheerful song filling me with a small sense of hope.

Were things looking up for me?

Was this chance meeting with Mr. Weird-Accent the start of something new?

I'd left my house in total despair, ignoring the family car and choosing to walk instead. I caught the bus and stayed on there until I reached Santa Monica. It was a freaking long trip from Pasadena, but thankfully Angel slept, and I had a chance to bring my tears under control.

I walked to the beach once I got off the bus, ambling along the upper walkway and looking out over the ocean. Being a winter weekday, it wasn't exactly crowded. There had been one jogger running near the water's edge and a few families with young kids playing. I loved it over that side of town, far away from my past. Angel had woken mid-morning, and I'd stopped at a park bench and given her a little snack. I was still damn tired, and it was tempting to lie down and rest right there...like a homeless person.

It somehow felt fitting. I did feel homeless.

I was hindering my sister's life by living at home. Dad obviously didn't want me there. The best solution was to move out, but where the hell was I supposed to go?

The song crescendoed for its final chorus, and as

soon as it came to an end, I selected it again. Jason Mraz had such an amazing voice; that alone was enough to make me feel better, but this song. I felt like it'd been designed just for me, for this moment.

That guy had totally nailed it.

Was it some kind of divine intervention?

Was that what had brought me to the community notice board?

After Angel's snack and a little Army-style crawling on the grass, I'd strapped her back against me and we'd wandered the area for a few hours, my spirits deflating with each step. Finally I'd come to a stop at the board, unable to take another step.

Exhaustion had me crying like a little baby. I thought I'd die of embarrassment when that guy approached with his carefree swagger and that beanie perched on the top of his head. I don't know how he did it, but this cool vibe just seemed to pulse out of him. I think it was the dull, gray beanie and the buds in his ears. It wasn't hard to tell he was a creative type...my kind of people. At least I *used* to be like that, until I had a baby and lost myself completely.

I should have scuttled away the second he came to stop beside me, but I couldn't move. Fatigue had planted my feet in the concrete and let tears roll down my face in spite of the company.

Thankfully, he'd been nice about it.

I glanced up the road again. He was out of sight now. I wondered what his name was.

He seemed sweet, had kind eyes and a smile to

match. I stepped over to the notice he'd pinned on the board, wondering what he was looking for.

FURNISHED APARTMENT FOR RENT
Top-floor apartment, five blocks from the beach.
Two bedrooms, one bathroom.
Contact Leo for further information: 424-331-4659

My insides skittered as I read the notice.

"Leo," I whispered, and before common sense could stop me, I lifted my phone and snapped a quick shot of the notice.

The song came to an end and I selected it again. Angel wiggled against me, a sure sign she would be waking soon. I checked the time on my phone. She'd be ready for another feed when she woke, and it was probably time I headed back home to tidy my room and make sure dinner was on. I wanted to do some laundry, too, because I *did* actually know how to separate colors and whites!

The idea of returning was like a stone in my gut, but it wasn't as heavy as it had been that morning.

I had an out now. Sitting on my phone was a number that could be the answer to my problem.

It hadn't even occurred to me at the time that there was no way in Hades I could afford to rent a two-bedroom apartment in Santa Monica. All I could focus on was the fact that maybe, just maybe, things were looking up.

NINE

LEO

The lyrics still weren't coming. I usually wrote lyrics and music together, couldn't really do one without the other, but not this time. I had a few melodies I was falling in love with, just no words. The tunes were growing a little more each day, and I could hear the orchestra behind them as I tinkered away at the piano.

But I hadn't found my theme yet.

My mind kept walking back to Blue Eyes at the community notice board. Because of her tears, the aqua color in her eyes had been so vibrant and strong. That hopeless look on her face...

I shook my head, hoping the song had worked.

Scratching at my stubble, I figured I should probably think about shaving in the morning, but for now, I wanted to nail this piece. The pads of my fingers sat lightly on the ivory keys, my middle finger resting on F-sharp as I worked in the key of D.

"Come on, inspiration, hit me," I muttered.

I was blaming the busyness of looking after the building for my lack of progress with the musical. That was why I wanted to let the empty apartment across the hall. Bobby had actually given me the entire top floor—both apartments—saying I could use the smaller one as a music studio, but I didn't need much living space, so I moved all my stuff into the small one with the idea of renting out the two-bedder and making myself some cash. Then, I could hire someone to help me. An assistant could look after the general running of the building, and I could spend more time composing.

Bobby said I needed something spectacular and unique for him to pitch to his guy in NYC.

"It's gonna have to be pretty damn amazing, Leo, or my guy won't even give you a look in."

I'd assured him I could pull it off. Bobby had given me a really great deal through a connection of his, and I'd managed to get all the gear at total mate's rates. I'd saved myself thousands. On top of that, Bobby had surprised me with a pristine second-hand baby grand. It took over my living space, but I didn't care. All my best creating happened on the real thing. I only used the electronic stuff when I wanted to record something.

I wriggled in my seat and played a D-chord. The lid of the piano was propped open an inch, and the rich sound made me smile. My fingers took control and sped up the keyboard, the tinkling sound filling me with a familiar sense of peace.

Music made everything better.

The phone on the counter rang. I always hated walking away from the piano when I was playing, but I jumped up and grabbed it, hoping it'd be someone calling about the apartment. I didn't recognize the number, so that was a good sign.

"Hello?" I sat back down on the piano stool and crossed my fingers.

"Um, hi, yeah, hey, um..." The female voice was soft. There was a girly sweetness to it that was plain adorable. "I'm just calling about the apartment for rent."

"Oh, great. I was hoping I'd get a quick response. I only pinned the notice up this afternoon."

"Yeah." She cleared her throat. "How much would it be?"

"Three thousand a month."

She hissed, a sharp intake of breath that told me this wouldn't be a goer.

"Not good, aye? I've done my research, and that's actually below market standard for a two-bedroom place. I mean, it's a small apartment, so I'm trying to be fair."

"Yeah, there's no way I can afford that." She sighed. "If I'm honest...I don't know why I'm even calling. I'm a single mother with no income because my baby's still little and I just..." She sighed again and then gave a dry chuckle. "I guess I'm desperate for a change of scenery."

I paused, my eyebrows bunching together. "Hang on a sec, you're not that girl I met at the notice board this afternoon, are ya?"

"Yeah. Yeah, I am."

I grinned. "Did the song work?"

Her reply took a moment to come, but finally she said, "Yes, it did. Thank you. I've been listening to it all evening."

Geez, that made me feel good. "What's your name?" I ran my finger gently over middle C.

"Jody."

"I'm Leo."

"Hi." I could hear the smile in her voice, but it faded when she cleared her throat. "Well, I'm sorry for wasting your time. I'm trying to figure out ways to earn a little cash while still looking after my baby, but I don't think any amount of cleaning houses or whatever could pay for your apartment."

Cleaning houses. Her words lit an idea hiding in the corner of my brain. I bit the edge of my lip and then started talking before I could stop myself. "I'll tell you what, how about this..."

Leo, what the hell are you doing?

Running my tongue over my lower lip, I ignored my inner voice.

"The reason I'm trying to rent out the apartment is that I need a little income. You see, I'm the building manager, and it's taking up quite a bit of time. Time I'd rather use for other things, so I figured if I could sublet the apartment across the hall from me, score myself a little extra cash, then I could maybe split the job with someone else and pay them to work part-time."

"That makes sense."

"So..." *Leo, don't be an idiot!* "What if I offered you the apartment for free and you could by my assistant."

She was taken aback; I could tell by the sudden pause. I was getting good at catching this girl off-guard. Hell, I was catching myself off-guard with this one. What was I thinking, offering a job to some chick I'd only just met? But her eyes...those tears. I wanted to help her.

She chuckled, a breathy, disbelieving one. "You'd let me live in your two-bedroom apartment for free?"

"Well, I'd be asking you to help manage the building. It's a busy job. You'd be dealing with tenants, organizing fix-it type stuff, maintaining the general upkeep of the building, that type of thing. Housekeeping for the two apartments we rent out on a short-term basis and then a regular clean for Ms. Thornby." I paused, waiting for her reaction. She didn't give me one, so I kept talking. "It might be a good job for you, you know, 'cause you could work from home and your little baby could be with you for the day."

"You wouldn't mind me taking my daughter with me for all that stuff?"

"Of course not! I'm sure she won't be any

trouble, will she?"

"No, she's only eight months old, she's fine."

"So, is that a yes?" Why did I sound so hopeful? This was an awful idea!

"Okay, but how would I earn any money? I mean, I still need to feed two mouths and, you know, buy diapers and stuff."

"Well." I chewed on the inside of my cheek as I thought, berating myself yet again for being so foolhardy on this thing, but it felt right. I mentally flipped the bird at my cautious warnings and went for it. "What about this...I give you twenty percent of my current wage plus free food and housing."

"You'd pay for my food?"

"Maybe we could include doing my grocery shopping in your job description and you get what you need for yourself at the same time. Sound good?"

"Actually, it sounds perfect. Like, too good to be true."

I grinned. "I'm serious. Why don't you swing by tomorrow and you can check out the place, see if you like it. I'll draw up some kind of contract and we can make this official."

"Okay." Her chuckle sounded lighter.

I gave her the address and hung up, throwing the phone onto the two-seater couch behind me. Mate, I felt good! My fingers trilled over the keys, and then I let out a laugh while I found the right chords and started singing "I Feel Good."

TEN

JODY

It wasn't hard to find Leo's building. His directions had been clear. I'd borrowed the family car, dropping Morgan off at the dance studio on my way so I could have it. She asked me where I was off to and I hedged, saying Angel and I needed a day out. I told her we were heading to the beach for some winter sunshine. She bought it with a smile, giving me a kiss on the cheek as she got out of the car.

My nerves were buzzing as I made my way to Santa Monica. I liked the area; I actually worked there when I was pregnant with Angel. Not wanting to bump into any of my school friends from Pasadena, I spent as much time in hiding as I could. Taking a job at a grocery store in the area kept me busy and away. It worked...and it was time to get away again.

I parked the car across the street and looked up at the red, brick building. It was pretty plain from the outside, just a big old rectangle with the front entrance smack in the middle, like a mouth. I felt like I was looking at the kind of apartments you'd find in a children's picture book. I guessed it was old and had been renovated.

Unbuckling Angel's straps, I lifted her onto my hip and grabbed the diaper bag. Man, I'd be glad to get rid of the thing once she'd outgrown it. When was that? Three years away? I tried not to cringe.

Checking the street, I crossed and headed up the stairs. My good vibes were battling it out with my negative nerves. I still couldn't believe Leo's offer. It was so original it almost didn't seem possible. Could I seriously manage a building?

I waited for the old elevator to crank its way down to us. The place felt a little rickety, but the paint on the walls was fresh and clean. I pressed six and we rode to the top. As soon as the doors dinged open, I stepped out into a small hallway, made bright and airy by a skylight in the ceiling. Opposite me were a set of stairs leading down, and on either side were two pale brown doors encased in white framework. I stepped to my left and knocked once, clutching Angel closer to me as we listened to the sounds behind the wood.

"Coming!"

I grinned; there was that accent again. So funny.

"I wonder where he's from," I whispered to Angel.

She replied with a cheerful little "Goo!" and then started slapping lightly at my face.

I grabbed her fingers and pretended to eat them, which had her squealing with a high-pitched giggle that made me wince.

The door flew back and there stood Leo. He looked different clean-shaven—younger, fresher, although maybe not as handsome. He kind of suited the light stubbly look, not that I cared either way. He wasn't really my type. I preferred sharp, precise perfection...like Stefan. Leo was a total contrast with his dark locks of unkempt hair, low-slung jeans, and wrinkled T-shirt.

I was distracted from my silent assessment by his smile. It was still the same with or without facial hair, so broad it took over his entire face. Oh, and in this light his eyes looked green. That was kinda nice.

"G'day."

So his accent was adorable. I had to give him that.

I hoisted Angel higher onto my hip and smiled. "Hi."

"And who's this little one?" He leaned toward my daughter, bending down so their heads were level.

"This is Angelia."

Leo hummed the chorus of Richard Marx's

"Angelia," and I nodded with a smile. "That's right."

He winked at me and then turned his attention back to Angel.

"Hey, cherry blossom. You are just all kinds of cute, aren't you?" He wiggled her foot, which made her giggle again. He laughed with her and gently tousled the fuzz on her head. "She's beautiful."

"Thank you." My heart swelled at his compliment. I could see how much he meant it. It was a relief to know he was good with kids. I wanted my neighbor to be understanding. When Angel really got going, her cries and screams could be damn piercing...and they were only getting louder as she grew bigger.

"Let me show you the place." Leo left his door open and walked across the hall, pulling a key from his pocket and unlocking it for us. He swung the door open and stepped aside so Angel and I could walk through.

My lips parted as I entered the light oasis. Skylights made up the roof over the living area, creating a sunny, warm atmosphere.

"Apparently it can get pretty hot in the summer, but there's good AC through the whole building, so as long as you leave it on, you should be all right." Leo crossed his arms, and I couldn't help noticing the way his biceps curved. He seemed like one of those guys who was oblivious to his strength.

I looked away from him and studied the open-plan living and kitchen area. The kitchen was small, yet workable. An island separated the kitchen from the living room. It was a counter/breakfast bar type deal with two stools on the other side of it. The floors were wooden throughout with a big Indian-style rug in the center, held in place by a three-seater futon. There was a low coffee table in front of it and a long, low bookshelf against the wall.

"Sorry there's no TV, I don't really watch much."

"No, that's cool. I've got my computer."

He nodded. "Ah, rooms are down this way." He pointed behind him, and we followed him around the corner. He was right; the place was small. The hallway was a storage closet long and then there was the master bedroom, which housed a double bed, one side table, and a set of drawers. Opposite that was a smaller bedroom/office space with a desk and chair, and between the two rooms sat a bathroom.

"Oh, good, there's a bathtub."

"Yeah, no separate shower, but I bought a new curtain last week." He pointed to the dark green curtain with pale green leaves dotted across it.

"Nice," I murmured.

Angel was kicking her little legs, trying to wriggle out of my grasp. "One sec, Angel."

"You want to explore, don't ya?" Leo chuckled at her.

I walked back through to the living area and set Angel down on the carpet, watching her carefully as she dropped forward and did a jerky crawl toward the tassels on the edge of the rug.

"So, what do you think? Are you—?" Leo's question was cut short by a ringing phone from his apartment. "Sorry, one sec."

He darted out of the room. I folded my arms and scanned the space, picturing Angel and I living here.

Could I seriously do this?

Could I take care of Angel and live by myself? Cook meals? Do laundry? Help look after a building?

Fear and doubt clawed at me, restricting my airways. I squeezed my eyes shut.

"Stop it, Jody!" I muttered. "You *can* do this."

Yeah, it'd be hard, but I could.

I didn't *need* Morgan and Dad to cope. I was capable of raising my baby and carving out a life for myself. It may not have been the one I planned on, but it would be okay.

A tune came to me, swelling in my stomach and pushing at my voice box. I opened my mouth and set it free, singing one of my favorite songs from the musical *Wicked*—"Defying Gravity."

It seemed appropriate somehow. I was taking a leap, pushing aside all my doubts and going for it, knowing it could end up being an epic fail, but believing that maybe, just maybe, it wouldn't be.

Angel glanced up from the tassel she was trying to suck on. She was on her belly; dribble hanging from her bottom lip. I grinned at her, my voice rising as I spread my arms wide and felt that old euphoric buzz zip through me.

ELEVEN

LEO

I spent most of the phone call assuring Bobby that I was making the right decision. I was lying through my teeth, of course.

"Yeah, mate, I'm telling you, she's totally qualified. She does have a kid, but it won't be a problem. We've worked out an agreement that suits us both."

Bobby sighed. "Have you interviewed her properly?"

"Come on, Bobby. How hard is it to do this job, I mean really?"

"Do not let her sign that contract until you know

a little more about her background."

"I won't." I rolled my eyes, knowing I probably would. How could I say no now? If she wanted the place, it was hers.

"I just don't want her moving in expecting some kind of free ride or something."

"I really don't think that's the case. Besides, what's the worst that can happen? If it doesn't work out, we'll just ask her to leave. We've covered ourselves with that six-week trial period. You looked over the contract this morning, and I've made those tweaks you suggested. It's all good."

"Yeah, yeah, okay. I guess there is that out clause with the whole six-week thing. Just make sure you keep an eye on her."

I grinned; I couldn't imagine that being a problem.

The pleasure of that idea took me by surprise. I jolted upright and shook it from my head.

"Scan the contract through to me once it's signed."

"Got it."

I hung up, snatching the documents off the counter and walking back across the hall.

The sound of her pure voice cresting over the lyrics of "Defying Gravity" stopped me dead in my tracks. Bloody hell, she sounded *amazing*.

I paused in the doorway, utterly entranced. She was standing in the kitchen, her arms spread wide, a massive smile on her face. She looked like sunshine and sounded like a nightingale. My mouth dropped open in awe, my eyes popping wide. The way she held her long notes with such sweet beauty enchanted me.

She dropped her arms and spun, opening her mouth to crescendo into the final chorus...and spotted me.

Her lips smacked together and she cringed, her cheeks heating with color as she scratched her right eyebrow.

"Don't stop, please. That was beautiful." I stepped into the room.

She grinned and mouthed, "Thank you."

"No, I mean, that was seriously magnificent. Why aren't you on a stage?"

Her smile fled, her eyes darting to the little baby playing on the floor. "I was studying performing arts last year, but things have been put on hold."

My heart sank for her; the sadness in her voice told me everything she couldn't say.

As much as I wanted to learn more, I couldn't stand the crestfallen look on her face; it was mixed with a humiliation I knew all too well.

Screw the interview. Bobby would just have to take my gut instinct as proof.

I cleared my throat and walked up to the counter, placing the contract down.

"So, why don't you have a read through this."

"Okay, thanks." She pulled it toward her and I got busy entertaining Angel. Sitting cross-legged in front of her, I used my best Uncle Leo voice and coaxed a quick smile out of her. She chattered back to me, making a string of unintelligible sounds that were lyrical and sweet.

"You trying to sing like your mummy, aye?"

She rocked back on her bottom, nearly toppling over. I caught her and pulled her back upright and she kept going, the sweet babble making me grin.

"She loves music, too," Jody murmured, her eyes still on the contract.

"It's food for the soul."

Jody paused and looked down at me, a smile pushing at her lips before she resumed reading.

Ten minutes later, she asked for a pen.

"So, you're all good with everything?"

She nodded. "All good. I can't see anything that needs changing. I like the job description. It's a really good deal, Leo. Thank you." Her sincere gratitude was endearing. "Are you sure you're happy for me to do this?"

"Yeah, well, there's the six-week trial, so we should be sweet, right? I mean, we've both got an out if we need it."

"Yeah, that sounds good." Her head bobbed. She pressed her lips together, the pen wiggling in her fingers before she lurched forward and quickly signed her name. Her writing was fluid and twirly, just like I imagined it would be.

When she was done, I spun it around and signed my own name, handing her a copy before folding mine in half and shoving it in my back pocket.

"Well, I look forward to you moving in next week."

"Thanks, me too." She stepped around me and collected Angel into her arms. "This is going to be a great home for us."

She was still unsure; I could tell by the waver in her voice, but I got why. I'd spotted her birth date on the contract. She was only twenty. This young thing had been thrown into adult shoes before she was even ready for it. I didn't know her very well, but I could see she was trying to make the most of it, which only impressed me more.

I helped her downstairs, holding the baby bag while she buckled Angel into her carseat. I made sure to get one more squealing laugh out of the girl before closing her door and opening Jody's.

"You're good with kids." She smiled as she pushed the key into the ignition.

My nose wrinkled the way it always did when people gave me compliments. "I have nieces and nephews back home. I lived with them for a short while." I nearly said more but went for a shrug instead. I'd actually used Kev's heart attack as a reason to move out of home with Gerry and shift in to help Deb with the kids. I'd convinced myself they'd needed me there full-time to cope, and in a way they had, but everyone knew it was just an excuse.

Jody buckled up and slid on her shades before glancing at me. "Where is home?"

"Here, at the moment." I winked.

Her head tipped, and I could tell she was giving me a dry look behind those sunglasses.

I chuckled. "Sydney, Australia."

"Wow, cool." She started the car with a nod, and I took the chance to close her door and wave goodbye. As much as she didn't want to tell me the details of dropping out of college, I didn't want to tell her about why I left my home country.

I had no idea where she currently lived and why she was leaving, but maybe we didn't need to know about each other's histories to work together.

I liked the idea of a fresh slate with my new assistant. The less we knew, the better.

TWELVE

JODY

The suitcases were open on the bed, clothes strewn across the floor, and two half-packed boxes lay next to Angel's crib. Ella had Angel for the afternoon as Reynolds, the bar restaurant she owned with her boyfriend, Cole, was having a lighter day. She rang me that morning on the spur of the moment and asked if I needed a breather.

"How about I take Angel for you?"

The offer had been such a relief, I burst into tears and spilled the beans to my best friend. I hadn't told another soul. I knew that was stupid. I mean, like Morgan and Dad wouldn't notice me leaving, but I just wanted to be packed and ready to go before they found out.

Thanks to my petite bestie, I'd had the day to myself. It was a relief to realize I really didn't need that much stuff, just everything from my room, the stroller from downstairs, and the carseat. I couldn't take the car; Morgan needed it for work, and since I was going to be living where I worked, I figured I could either bus or walk. I still wanted the carseat, though, and today was a prime example of why. Ella had been forced to take Angel out in the stroller because Morgan had the car, and we had no way to safely transport my baby.

I had no idea where they'd ended up, but I knew they'd be safe. Ella was the sweetest person on the planet, proved by the fact that half an hour after I told her my plan, her boyfriend called and offered to help move my stuff.

I nearly cried the words 'thank you'. The towering hunk just laughed. "It's never a problem, Jody."

Of all the couples in the world, Ella and Cole were the best. I knew they were probably worried about me making this big decision, but they were supportive anyway.

I feared I wouldn't get the same reaction from my family.

The front door clicked open downstairs. I tensed, waiting to hear Ella's greeting. It never came, and my muscles wound that little bit tighter.

"Hello? Is anybody home?"

Oh, shit! It was Dad.

I steeled myself, pulling in a breath as I folded my pants and shoved them into the suitcase.

"Jody?" He peeked his head into my room and froze. "What are you doing?"

"Packing." I kept my words short. I didn't want to get into it. I knew he'd pretend to be shocked at my decision, but deep down he wanted me out of here. It'd be easier for everyone.

He crossed his arms, his stocky frame filling the doorway. "And where do you think you're going?"

I kept my eyes on my clothes and attempted to steady my voice. It didn't work.

"I've found an apartment in Santa Monica." I dared a glance in his direction.

Dad's head jolted back, giving him a double chin. "And how are you going to pay for that?"

"With the job I also got."

His jaw worked to the side, his voice like concrete. "What are you doing with Angel?"

It was hard not to get rattled, so I kept my hands busy and my sentences short. "I'll be working from my new apartment. She can be there with me."

"What is this job?" His eyes narrowed as he stepped into the room.

I threw my last pair of pants into the bag and flipped the lid shut. "Building manager. I'm going to be looking after the tenants of the apartment building I'm moving into."

Dad's face wrinkled with doubt, and I spoke before he could tell me how stupid I was.

"I can do it, Dad. The job description fits my skill set, and I signed the contract a couple of days ago. I'm moving in tomorrow."

"Tomorrow? When were you going to tell us about this?"

"Tomorrow." My voice was small.

"Jody..." Dad closed his eyes, shaking his head with that disappointed look on his face.

Anger burned.

"I know you think stupidity is my MO right now, but I've thought this through, and it's the right decision for everybody."

"What's the right decision?" Morgan appeared in the doorway, her tall, curvaceous frame making Dad look short and round beside her. He was only half an inch shorter than his eldest daughter, but the effect was kind of comical.

She took in my messy, half-packed room with a frown, her umber gaze landing on the crib. "Where's Angel?"

"With Ella." I rubbed a finger under my nose. Damn that it was shaking!

"What's going on?" Morgan's voice was quiet, but I knew it wouldn't stay that way for long.

"Jody's moving out!" Dad pointed at me. "Got herself a job and is taking Angel with her!"

"What? Wh-when!" My sister always looked so funny when she was flabbergasted I would have laughed if it hadn't been for the hard expression on Dad's face.

He wouldn't make eye contact, just kept scanning the room and shaking his head. You know what, screw him! If he didn't want to man-up and talk to me about this stuff, then that was his problem. I didn't have to talk to him, either. I wanted to yell at him to get out, but I didn't have to. He flicked his hands in the air as if he was done with me and walked out of the room.

Morgan stayed.

Unfortunately.

Her hands were planted firmly on her hips, and it was in moments like this that she moved from the friend corner smack back into the sister zone.

"Why are you doing this?"

I hefted one of the boxes off the floor and dumped it on the bed, emptying my bedside cabinet and deciding to go for the truth.

"I can't live here anymore. I feel like I've lost all my joy. I'm sick of moping around this house feeling sorry for myself. It's time to get out of here and figure out what I need to make me happy. Living in this negativity is killing me."

"What negativity?"

I threw a small stack of books into the box and spun. "Oh, come on! I know what you guys think of me! Dad can't even look me in the eye anymore. I screwed up! And he's never going to let me forget it!"

Morgan's long fingers smoothed back the curls trying to pop free of her short ponytail. "Dad just struggles to deal with his emotions. You know what he's like. But he loves you...and Angel. We don't want you to move out."

"Yes, you do," I mumbled, kicking at the floor with my toe. "If I wasn't here, you would have said yes to Sean's proposal and you'd be living with him now. I'm holding you back."

"I don't—" Morgan's frown was sharp. "How do you know about that?"

"I heard you talking in the kitchen."

"Oh, you mean the day you took off without telling anybody?"

"I texted you." I rolled my eyes.

Morgan straightened her back and lifted her chin. She always did that when she was feeling antsy, fighting to stay strong. "Jo-Jo, you're not holding me back. I like helping you raise Angel."

My hip jutted to the side as I crossed my arms and threw her a dry look.

She gave me a sheepish grin. "Hey, she's my niece and she's adorable...and you're my sister."

"Yes, your sister, not your daughter." I kept my voice soft, knowing Morgan's face would fall with my words. I'd only been ten when Mom left and Morgan had been forced to fill the gap. I would have fallen apart without her, but the truth still remained—she wasn't anyone's mother, but I was.

I licked my lower lip. "I'm not your responsibility, Morgan, but Angel is mine. My only priority is keeping her safe and happy, and in order to do that, I need to be happy, too. Give me a chance to prove that I can be everything she needs me to be." I stepped forward and took Morgan's arms. "I need you to believe in me."

I could tell that would be a struggle. Morgan was so used to being in control and organizing everybody. She was good at it, a total pro, and I'd always taken advantage of her motherly spirit, but it was time to spread my wings.

"Are you sure you're going to be okay? I mean, there's so much you're gonna have to do, and I don't know anything about this situation. How am I going to help you?"

"You're not." I squeezed her arms. "I'm going to do this on my own."

She frowned.

"It's okay. I know what I'm doing."

Total lie.

I mean, I did, but her doubts were giving me a major case of the jitters. I'd been so confident telling Ella this morning, but that's because Ella was telling me how awesome I was. She was Miss Encouragement. Morgan, on the other hand, was Miss Practicality, and the doubt on her face tore straight through me.

Crap! How much did she do already that I didn't know about it?

I wanted to drop to my knees and beg for a detailed list.

Give me everything you've got!

But I couldn't, because then she'd see how useless I really was, and like hell I was admitting to that.

No, this was me defying gravity and wishing on every star in the sky that I didn't come tumbling down with an almighty crash.

The last time I'd gone out on my own, I'd come home pregnant, my dreams trailing behind me in tatters.

I couldn't let that happen again, because this

time I had another human being to consider, a sweet, precious Angel that I'd rather die than hurt in any way. The sad reality was, if I fell, she'd come plunging down beside me.

THIRTEEN

LEO

Jody moved in three weeks ago...and things had been going well. I saw her a lot in that first week as I ran through her job description and showed her what I wanted. She was really receptive and listened intently. From what I could tell, she'd been following through on everything. I hadn't had to chase her up and I knew this, because I hadn't seen her in over a week.

I'd been stuck at my piano while inspiration flowed through me like water. It struck the day I saw her singing in the kitchen, her arms spread wide with that blissful expression on her face. She was my nightingale, my muse, and that one image of her singing about starting over and taking a leap sparked an idea so potent I hadn't been able to escape it. Because of her, I had the start to my musical. Lyrics and compositions had been pouring out of me as I worked through Act I, confident I was onto something good.

I cleared my throat and sang the first line of "I Want The World," my voice dipping and rising over the notes. The melody was like a roller-coaster ride, but it suited the piece. The main character's emotions were all over the place as fear and trepidation battled it out with an excitement so strong and liberating she felt like she could fly.

My nose wrinkled as I played the next note.

"That's not going to work, mate," I mumbled to myself, leaning forward with my eraser and rubbing out my messy notes on the upper staff. Yes, I was old school. I liked to compose Mozart style and transfer my work to digital after it was done. It took longer, but I didn't care. I wasn't going to let technology hamper my creative flow.

I fiddled with the melody until I found that sweet note, matched with the perfect minor chord to let it really soar. Whoever sang that line would hold it steady, drawing in the audience with a sound that would hopefully make their spirits rise.

I could picture Jody on the stage, a yellow spotlight surrounding her as she sang about chasing down every single one of her dreams.

I played the line again, trying not to let the image force me into a mistake. It was pretty bloody distracting, that's for sure. I closed my eyes and shook my head. Clearing my throat yet again, I went for it.

My long note was cut short by the ringing phone.

I swore and stood from the stool, hating the interruption. But when I saw the number, I couldn't help a grin. Godfather Bobby.

"Hey, mate, how's it going?"

"Pretty good, son. I was just ringing to check in on your new employee."

"She's doing great." I shrugged, hoping I was right. This conversation was reminding me that Bobby had asked me to do weekly check-ins during the trial period. I'd been too distracted and totally forgotten. No tenants had complained, so I figured everything was running smoothly.

"How'd her last check-in go?"

"Really well," I lied. "She's a good little cleaner. Ms. Thornby hasn't complained at all."

"Wow! That's impressive."

I chuckled. "Tell me about it."

"She remembering to record any financial stuff and keep a written record of everything?"

"You betchya." Another lie. I really had no idea and needed to follow-up on that.

"And she's coping okay with looking after her baby and staying on top of the workload?"

"Seems to be doing just fine."

"Well, that's good news. I'm gonna swing by next week and have a chat with her, make sure she's still enjoying the job."

"She is, mate. You don't need to worry."

"Okay. That's cool. Listen, before you go, I've had something come up and I thought of you."

"Oh, yeah? What's that?"

"A friend of mine is selling off an old, run-down theater close to you guys. It's been out of action for over a decade, and I want to help him out, so I've offered to buy it. I was wondering if you'd be interested in resurrecting it for me."

My eyebrows rose.

"I mean, it'd be no Broadway or anything, more like a cute little local theater. You could put on a couple of productions a year, draw a small a crowd. Heck, you could even use students who are studying acting so you wouldn't have to pay them much. I'd front the money and you'd be paid from any profits once I'd broken even...and of course, you'll still get your current wage as building manager until the place is up and running."

I nodded.

"I figured since Jody is basically running things for you now, you could put your time into that instead. It'd be a good way for me to make your working visa more legit, and you'd be your own boss, really run the thing the way you want to."

My lips pursed to the side.

"So what do you think?"

"Uh, it sounds pretty good, but...I've still got my sights set on Broadway, mate. I'm really after the big time."

Bobby made a tutting noise. "I understand, I just can't guarantee you that. I still haven't managed to pin down my contact in New York."

"Yeah, I know, mate, but I'm not ready to give up yet. I'm working on something really good, and I feel like this could be my only shot. I want to spend my time perfecting this musical, not refurbishing a run-down theater."

"Yeah, well, it would be a lot of work."

I chewed my lip, those old fears surfacing. Maybe I should take it. My chances for Broadway were so pathetically slim anyway. Was I being an idiot to turn this opportunity down?

No! I'd come over here to chase my dreams. I'd regret it forever if I gave those up. I needed to fight for what I wanted, not what other people wanted me to do.

"All right." Bobby sighed. "But if you change your mind...or it doesn't work out, this could be your ticket. I'll leave the offer open for a few months while I try to find someone else. If I have no luck, I'll turn the building into something more sellable."

"Thanks for understanding. I think I'll regret it if I don't keep shooting for the stars while I can."

"You're pretty determined to make Broadway, aren't ya?"

"I don't think anything could stop me right now."

A scream from next door made me flinch. I jerked toward the sound, my eyes popping wide.

"Mate, I gotta go. Talk to you later."

I hung up before Bobby even said goodbye, lurching across my apartment and yanking the door open. The scream came again, loud and terrifying. My heart was bumping like a bloody jackhammer as I banged on Jody's door.

"Jody! You okay?"

"I can't move right now!" she yelled.

I tried turning the handle, but it was locked. "Are you hurt?"

"No, I just—I just—" She screamed again, making my blood run cold.

Charging back into my apartment, I yanked open the top kitchen drawer and scrambled for the spare set of keys. I dropped them as I leapt back into the hallway.

"Shit!" Snatching them back into my hand, I shoved the wrong one into the lock. Jody's scream made my belly quake. "Hang on!"

Finding the right key, I rammed it into the lock and tried to open the door, but as usual it stuck. Bloody hell! I had to get this damn door fixed! Shoving my shoulder into it, I punched it open with a loud grunt.

Jody was standing on the couch, her blue eyes wide and terrified. Angel was clutched against her chest, a crying, dribbling mess.

"What is it?" I ran toward them.

"Sp—sp—" She was out of breath, her finger shaking as she pointed to the floor. "Spider!" She screamed again.

I couldn't help my ridiculous frown as I turned and watched a spider playing at the base of the coffee table, its long legs flirting with the wood.

"Kill it, kill it! KILL IT!"

Her shouting made me jerk and I spun to her, an incredulous look no doubt plastered on my face.

She gave me a shaky smile. "I mean, please kill it."

Tears hovered on the edges of her lashes, her gaze darting back to the floor. She flinched, her mouth dropping open with a gasp.

I glanced back down and the spider had gone. I thought Jody might pass out. The only thing stopping her from keeling over was the screaming baby in her arms.

She bobbed Angel on her hip, absentmindedly patting her back.

"It's okay, little one." I ran my knuckle gently down Angel's bright red cheek, wiping at a stream of tears. "Uncle Leo's going to get rid of the mean old spider, okay?"

I threw Jody a reproachful frown before bending to my knees and checking under the coffee table.

"There you are, you little critter."

Popping back up, I raised my hands and spoke slowly to the terrified woman on the couch. "It's okay, he's under the table. I'm just going to get a paper towel from the kitchen, and then I'll get rid of him for ya."

A tear popped free as she nodded. It was an effort not to tell her what I really thought. She was being bloody ridiculous! The spider could fit onto two quarters easily. It was hardly the biggest insect I'd ever seen. She'd bloody die if she came to Australia.

"Paper towels are by the—"

"Yeah, I see 'em." My eyes skittered over the kitchen as I reached for them. Dirty dishes were piled in the sink. A burnt piece of toast was propped up against the toaster, a half-eaten jar of baby food was sitting next to it and then sat a row of bottles, smelly formula still lining the interiors.

I forced myself not to comment as I made my way back into the lounge.

Thankfully the spider was still under the table and a slow little bugger, so I caught him easily, squishing him in the paper towel before searching the kitchen for the rubbish bin. Jody sucked in a breath as I lifted the overflowing bin lid and went to drop the remains inside. I glanced at her face and smiled.

"I'll throw this out at my place, shall I?"

She closed her eyes and stepped down off the couch, her foot landing in a pile of laundry. Clean or dirty? I wasn't sure.

Angel was still crying, but she was down to a hiccuping sniffle as opposed to a scream. I winked at the baby, making a clicking sound out the side of my mouth. Her eyes popped wide as she looked at me, her lips curving into a grin while a long dribble oozed from her mouth.

Jody wiped it with the back of her sleeve, then proceeded to wipe away her own tears.

"Sorry about that." She grimaced. "I'm not—It's a phobia I've had forever, and I know it's totally insane, but I can't control it. They just...they scare the crap out of me."

"It's all right." I smiled, wishing I hadn't given

her that reprimanding glare before. "Phobias are real. My sister-in-law is absolutely petrified of heights, freezes up like a statue. It took Kev over an hour to coax her down from a high-ropes course once."

"Why was she doing a high-ropes course?" Jody was horrified.

I shrugged. "She was trying to conquer her fear. Didn't work."

"Obviously." Jody huffed out a short, dry laugh.

She still looked pretty damn pale. It made the smudges under her eyes that much darker. "Are you sure you're okay? I can stick around if you need me to."

"Oh, no, that's fine." She waved her hand in the air. "I'm just gonna put Angel down for a nap and get cleaning." Her cheeks splashed red as she pointed to the kitchen and then over her shoulder to the living area. I think a whirlwind must have passed through. "I'm a little behind today."

Just today? Some of the mess seemed kind of stale. How did she live like this? I'd be out of my tree trying to function in this kind of chaos.

"Yeah, yeah, no worries." I nodded, giving her what I hoped was an encouraging smile as I said goodbye and let myself out. I turned to look at her one more time before I left.

Her shoulders were hunched, and I noticed her swipe at one more tear as Angel's fussing increased in volume.

With a small frown, I closed the door gently and headed back to my piano.

Maybe Jody wasn't coping as well as I thought she was.

FOURTEEN

JODY

Okay, so the spider thing was freaking embarrassing. Not to mention the state of my apartment. I didn't miss the slightly shocked expression on Leo's face. I could have died.

I wanted to give my boss a good impression, and there I was screaming over a spider, ignoring how much my reaction was terrifying Angel...and then the mess. Aw, man, the mess!

"Seriously, Jody, you're useless!" It'd been a week since my utter humiliation, and I still hadn't gotten over it. I couldn't even look at Leo when he came to do his weekly check-in the day before, and

I actually chickened out this morning and just dumped his groceries outside his door so I didn't have to face him.

It wasn't that he was being mean or anything, but the next time I saw him, I wanted to be able to look him in the eye and know that I was in full control.

"Like that's ever gonna happen!" I tutted, rinsing out yet another freaking baby bottle. I couldn't wait for Angel to be past this stage. I was so over washing copious amounts of plastic!

The only thing I did have going for me was that my duties as assistant building manager were running smoothly. I was keeping up with all maintenance requests, tenants seemed to like me, and the one short-term stay we'd had since I'd been working here went really well.

I was proud of myself for that, but it did mean I was falling behind on everything else. When I lived at home with Morgan and Dad, my only responsibility had been Angel and a little laundry, so it meant that when she napped, I could put my feet up, but that *never* happened anymore. It was so tempting to call it quits and move back home, but I couldn't do it. I'd hate myself forever.

And that look on Dad's face. UGH! Forget it!

I was going to make this work if it killed me.

The phone rang behind me. Flicking the water off my fingers, I dried my hands, glancing at the half-finished piece of toast on the kitchen counter. I had made that over two hours ago and still hadn't gotten back to it.

I could say one thing: this whole single parenting/working thing was definitely helping me shed my pregnancy weight. I never had time to eat; some days I'd get to lunch and realize I hadn't had breakfast yet. I'd been too busy to even feel hungry!

Glancing at the phone screen, I let out a loud sigh before pasting on a smile.

"Hi, Ms. Thornby. How are you today?"

"Not well. The man upstairs is making a terrible racket. I can't even hear what's going on in *The Bold and The Beautiful* and this is a very important episode!"

"The man upstairs from you?" I cringed, squeezing my eyes shut and praying she'd say no.

"Yes, Mr. Whatever-his-name-is. His TV is up so loud I can barely hear myself think. It's not fair! Why should I miss my show just because he's deaf? I need you to go and tell him to be quiet."

"Of course, Ms. Thornby. I'll deal with it right away."

"I should think so. Good luck, dear."

She hung up, and I placed the phone on the counter with a heavy sigh. Mr. Kransten. Apartment 3B. "Oh, joy," I mumbled, snatching the baby monitor and making sure it was working. I had tested it out in my first week, and thankfully it had a really good range, meaning I could leave Angel sleeping in her crib and not have to worry about missing her cries if she needed me.

Locking the door behind me, I muttered my way down the stairs, hoping Mr. Cray-Cray would go easy on me today. If he screwed up my six-week trial in any way, I'd be tempted to kill him. So far, I'd managed to keep all his annoying antics out from Leo's radar, but going down there to tell him off? The guy had already told me exactly what he thought of me, and he was not going to take kindly to this little visit.

Pasting on a cheery expression, I knocked on the door until my knuckles stung. That TV was ridiculously loud. I held my breath, hoping he heard me...and also kind of not.

"Please be nice this time," I whispered.

"What!" He threw back the door, barking at me like a police dog. The already-loud TV sounded a million times louder with the door ajar.

"Hello, Mr. Kransten!" I smiled. "I've had a concerned neighbor call me, saying there was a bit of noise coming from your apartment, and I was wondering if I could assist you in any way...like maybe helping you turn down the TV?"

"I don't need your help." He went to close the door in my face, but I held it open with my hand.

"Please, Mr. Kransten, part of your tenancy agreement is that you will respect your fellow neighbors, and your TV is way too loud. You need to turn it down."

He was a tall, spindly man with hardly a hair on his head. His beady eyes narrowed as he peered down his long nose at me. "And what are you going to do if I don't?"

"Do I really have to answer that question? I'm asking you nicely to turn it down."

"I can't, it's broken!" he barked again.

"Well, maybe I could take a look at it." I moved to step into the apartment, but he blocked my way.

"What makes you think I'm going to let a little kid into my house?"

I sighed. "Mr. Kransten, we've been over this before. I'm not a kid, and my job is assistant to the building manager. Please let me help you."

"I want to deal with a grown-up!"

It was impossible not to roll my eyes. "At least let me look at it, and we can go from there."

"Grown-up!" he yelled in my face before slamming the door shut.

I couldn't help a grunt of frustration as I stomped my foot and turned back up the stairs. I hated disturbing Leo. I didn't want to have to face him, yet again proving that I wasn't cut out for this job. But if I didn't swallow my pride, Ms. Thornby would be up my ass, and she'd make sure Leo fired me.

"Damn it." I stopped outside Leo's door and caught my breath, screwing up my face and knocking.

"Just a minute!"

I pinched my bottom lip as I waited for him, hating the sound of his lock clicking open.

"Hey." He smiled at me. He was wearing his pale green Quicksilver shirt today. I liked that one. "Everything okay?"

"Oh, ah, no, not really. I'm sorry, I don't mean to disturb you, but Mr. Cray-Cray is causing a disturbance on the third floor."

"Mr. Cray-Cray?" Leo's face wrinkled with confusion.

"Sorry, I mean Mr. Krantsen. I dubbed him a couple of weeks ago when he was yelling at the pigeons on his windowsill."

Thankfully Leo grinned, his green eyes dancing. I think that shirt made them look even greener.

"So, what's the problem today then?"

I sighed, flicking my hands in the air. "Apparently the volume on his TV is broken. The neighbors are complaining, and he's refusing to let me look at it for him. He said he wanted to speak to a grown-up." I lifted my eyes to the ceiling. "I should never have worn pigtails the day I went to introduce myself to everybody. I was going for sweet and friendly, like *Hey, I'm approachable.* What a total backfire," I ended with a mumble.

Leo chuckled. His smile was adorable, his barely there dimple showing beneath his short stubble.

I couldn't help a rueful grin as I scratched the top of my head. "I really hate bothering you over this, but he just won't deal with me."

"Don't worry about it. The guy's a sexist, old-school bastard. He treats me like a third-rate citizen, too." Leo grabbed his key off the hook beside the door and locked it behind him. "Let's go deal with the old grump together, aye?"

We headed downstairs, and of course Mr. K let Leo in immediately. He glared at me as I brought up the rear, probably because Leo had just reminded him that I was in charge of these matters and that I'd happily call a repairman if he wanted me to.

Mr. K just grunted and opened his door, stomping back into the living room.

His house smelled weird—old and stale. It matched him perfectly.

I wrinkled my nose and crossed my arms, resisting the urge to lean against the wall as Leo and Mr. Cray-Cray yelled at each other, competing against the insane volume of the TV. Leo started by trying to switch it off, but the TV was seriously screwed so he ended up unplugging it from the wall.

"What'd you do that for?"

"So we can hear ourselves think while we try to solve this problem." Leo placed his hands on his hips and turned back to the TV.

The silence didn't last long. A cry came through the baby monitor in my back pocket. I pulled it out to make sure I was hearing right. Yep, Angel was definitely up.

"I need to go, sorry."

Leo flicked his hand. "No worries."

Mr. K grunted in disgust, mumbling something. I didn't hear exactly what he said, but I was pretty sure the words "fire" and "hussy" were in there somewhere.

It frickin' stung.

I hurried out of the room, trying not to let it bother me, but I really couldn't help it. No wonder the old man hated me. All he saw was a young kid, stupid enough to get herself knocked up.

Bolting up the stairs, I let myself into the

apartment, willing the ugly feelings off me as I breezed into my baby's room.

"Hey, cupcake." I forced a sweet smile and lifted her from the crib, feeling those all-too-familiar tears brewing as I nestled her against me.

Damn it, Jody, not again!

Pull yourself together!

FIFTEEN

LEO

I wanted to punch Mr. Kransten in the gizzard for calling Jody a hussy and suggesting I fire her. What the hell was his problem? She worked her damn backside off to keep him happy, and it still wasn't good enough. He was a bigoted arsehole.

I couldn't fix the bloody TV. I wasn't a techy guy, and I didn't know what the hell was wrong with it.

"I'll get Jody to call a repairman this afternoon."

"I don't want to deal with her."

"Why?" I growled.

He crossed his arms, his chin pointing into the

air. "Any teenage girl fool enough to get herself pregnant is not capable of looking after a baby and running a building."

I pointed at him, willing my quivering limbs to stay put. "Now you listen to me, mate. Jody may be young, but she's doing a damn fine job running this place, and if you can't follow process and deal with her, you can bloody well move out!"

"I just might do that."

"Go ahead!" I stormed toward the door and turned back in time to see him reaching for the remote. "Don't even think about it!"

He dropped it onto the couch with a scowl and muttered, "I want a repairman here by the end of the day."

"Fine, I'll get *Jody* to call one right now."

I smiled at his black look before storming out the door and slamming it shut behind me. Muttering a string of obscenities, I took the stairs two at a time, pausing outside Jody's door to reel in my anger.

It didn't work; she heard me outside and swung the door open before I could contain myself.

Her face was blotchy, her eyes that vibrant blue color I'd seen before.

Shit, she'd been crying. Bloody Mr. Kranoten!

She had a jar of baby food in one hand, and her shirt was already smeared with a spoonful of it. A large curl had escaped her ponytail and curved across her left breast. I averted my gaze.

"Did you fix it?"

"No." I brushed past her, glancing at Angel in

her highchair before turning back to Jody, my eyes darting to that damn curl again. I spun away from her and waved at Angel, who kicked her legs and started babbling.

"So, what do you need me to do?" Jody walked back to her daughter, perching her perfect butt on the edge of a stool and attempting to get another spoonful of yellow slop into Angel's mouth.

"I told him you were going to call a repairman."

"Okay." She nodded, looking nervous.

Curse that man!

"But does he want me to do that, because if I show up with one I'm worried he won't let the guy in, and then if his TV doesn't get fixed, Ms. Thornby's going to complain again, and you know what she's like. I just..." She cringed. "Do you think he's right? I mean, should you fire me?"

I grunted and threw my hands in the air, hating that an old, wrinkly-faced, bald-headed *loser* could make a sunshine girl like Jody start doubting herself.

"That man's as thick as bloody pig shit if he thinks I'm going to fire you! And I've told him if he can't follow process then he can move out!"

A sudden burst of laughter made me turn. It was an explosion of colorful sound that sounded sweet to my ears. It only got better when Jody snorted, her eyes popping wide with horror as she slapped a hand over her mouth.

"What?" I found myself chuckling in spite of my confusion.

She dipped her head and tried to hide it, but

couldn't. Her shoulders started shaking and she held her nose, no doubt trying to ward off another snort.

"I'm sorry," she finally giggled the words. *"Thick as bloody pig shit.* That has got to be one of the funniest insults I've ever heard." She raised her hand in the air, her head shaking as the tip of her tongue popped between her teeth.

I chuckled, feeling my cheeks heat as I scratched the back of my neck.

Her laughter continued to float through the room like dancing butterflies. It was punctuated with a few quick intakes of breath and a lyrical sigh...and then her giggles would start all over again.

It sounded more like a hysterical release of emotion after the way Mr. Kransten had treated her, but I didn't care. It sounded beautiful.

My smile grew as Angel soon got into the action, doing a funny dance and banging her spoon on the highchair tray. Jody grinned at her, wiping some food slime off that chubby chin, her laughter finally dying down.

She cleared her throat as if embarrassed by her sudden outburst. Tucking that long curl behind her ear, she smiled at me. "I'll make some phone calls as soon as I've finished feeding Angel."

"Yeah, good, thanks." I headed for the door, my fingers suddenly burning for some piano keys. "Start with Mac. He's Bobby's go-to tech guy. I think his number's in the book I gave you."

"Okay." She grinned, looking lighter. Her

blotches were already fading.

"You're doing a great job, Jo. Don't let the Cray-Cray get to ya."

"Thanks." Her smile was sweet and endearing. I took a mental snapshot of the image back to my piano. Sitting down with a slight sense of awe, I played a G chord then shifted to D major. Yeah, that was it. Her sparkling laughter danced through my brain as my fingers took charge, recreating the melodic sound of Jody's laughter while another scene came to me—a lush green meadow filled with flowers and dancing butterflies.

SIXTEEN

JODY

"I passed!" I giggled into my phone, enjoying Ella's little cheer.

"Well done."

Man, I was glad she'd called. I'd needed a positive blip on my radar today and her calling to check in was exactly that.

"So they must be really pleased with your work then."

"Yeah, I mean, it's not like it was a test or anything, but Bobby popped over yesterday and okayed me to stay. I am now *officially* assistant to the building manager, in spite of Mr. Cray-Cray's complaints."

"Yeah, well Mr. Cray-Cray can go shove it where the sun don't shine." Ella's sweet voice saying that sentence was too funny.

I burst with laughter. "Listen to you, getting your Morgan on."

She giggled. "I try."

"You don't really pull it off." I wrinkled my nose.

"Shut up! I can do a Morgan!"

"You can try," I teased, enjoying the light banter between us. It was a nice reprieve from my totally shitty morning, and doing wonders to pull me out of my funk.

"Hey, sorry, Jo-Jo, I gotta go. Cole needs me."

And the funk was back.

"I'm sure he does." My suggestive innuendo lacked its usual luster, but Ella didn't seem to notice. I could imagine her blushing pink.

"Stop it." She put on a funny voice.

"Go on then, go get some."

She giggled, but didn't deny my assumption. With their late hours, Ella had confessed to often sneaking in some mid-morning nooky before the bar opened at lunchtime. When she'd first told me, I'd swooned at the romance of it all. Now it made me feel green.

I tried not to let the fact my lady parts were *out of service* bother me. If anything, I had to get used to the idea. I couldn't foresee any mid-day, mid-night, mid-*anything* nooky in my future.

Sucking in a breath, I pushed the depressing

reality aside and instead focused on the fact that it was a beautiful, sunny day and I was out strolling the Third Street Promenade. I loved this street—the shops, the cafes, the vibe. It was artsy and creative, and it made me feel just a little bit alive every time I came down here. It didn't take away my problems, but it helped me escape them for a while.

Angel had been awake most of the night. I had no idea what her problem was, but the after-effect of a lousy sleep had filtered into my day, turning me into a grumpy hag. I'd actually shouted at my baby girl. I rolled my eyes beneath my shades and cringed. She was snuggled into her stroller now, grinning up at me as if I hadn't turned all dragon-lady on her less than an hour ago.

"I only have two hands, Angel! I can't pick you up right now!" I'd screamed from the sink, desperately trying to finish cleaning the bathroom before I had to head downstairs to make sure the second guest apartment was ready for the next lot of short-term tenants. They were arriving that night.

She'd frozen on the floor, utterly shocked by my outburst. Her lower lip began quivering and her big eyes filled with tears before she elicited a feeble little cry that quickly grew with fervor and indignation.

I couldn't handle her wailing so I threw the rag into the sink and dried off my hands.

"Screw the apartment." I hefted her into my arms, grabbed the stroller, and we'd hit the sunshine. I could finish off the bathroom and the

115

guest apartment when we got back.

I gave Angel a rueful smile as she gazed up at me.

"Ma-ma-ma-ma!" She grinned, tapping her teething ring on the edge of the stroller.

I smiled in spite of myself, pushing the stroller forward and lifting my face to the sun.

Yeah, I could survive this day.

I jerked to a stop, my eyes catching on something.

Or maybe I couldn't.

My breath evaporated, my knuckles turning white on the stroller.

His lips parted when he saw me, his gaze unreadable behind his aviator shades. He paused, obviously unsure which way to turn, but I kept moving forward as if drawn by some gigantic magnet.

I stopped in front of him, the air in my lungs feeling dry and stale.

"Jody, hi."

"Hi, Stefan." I swallowed.

Shit, he looked good.

He slid his hands into his pockets. "What are you doing here?"

I shrugged. "Just out walking. How about you? I thought you'd be in Tucson right now."

His lopsided grin was delicious. I remembered exactly what it tasted like, my mouth filling with saliva at the very idea of kissing him again.

"I moved to LA in January. I scored myself a role in a Disney musical. It'll be showing at the

Walt Disney Concert Hall in April. If it goes well, they're going to take it over to Broadway. New York, here I come."

Okay, so his smile was becoming punchable. Damn that it still had a power over me, though. If he leaned forward, I wouldn't be able to resist. My autopilot would take over.

I leaned away from him. "Wow. Congratulations." Hot jealousy burned though my insides, but I forced a smile. "How'd you—how'd you get that role?"

"I got it for him." A sleek blonde appeared beside him. I had no idea where the hell she'd materialized from, but I instantly hated her. She was tall and lean, making me feel like a frumpy housewife. Except I wasn't anyone's wife! I was just a frumpy loser!

"My father owns the studio." The blonde girl smiled.

"Nice." I blinked, my head bobbing automatically before I gained control of it. My throat felt thick and swollen, but I forced my hand forward. "I don't think we've met."

"Selene." She grasped my hand with her long fingers. Her smile was kind and sweet. "I'm Stefan's fiancée."

My grip on her hand went slack, my eyes bugging out. Thank God I was wearing shades. They could still read my expression, though. I could tell by the way Stefan squirmed in his designer jeans.

What did I say to that?

Stefan was getting married? So I had his kid and I wasn't good enough for him? But she was?

Damn her! Damn him!

Angel, no doubt sensing my stress, started to fuss. I lifted her out of the stroller, more to settle her than anything, but I didn't miss Stefan's quick intake of breath.

Good! He should have to see her, come face to face with what he threw away.

Selene's face lit with an enchanted smile as I spun Angel around.

"Oh, hello." She put on that high voice adults use when talking to babies. "And who are you?"

I kept my eyes on Stefan, saw that little shake of his head and decided to ignore the hell out of it.

Pasting on a plastic smile, I introduced my little girl. "This is Angel, Stefan's daughter, but I'm guessing he hasn't told you about her yet, because he likes to pretend that she doesn't exist."

Selene shot back, her eyes darting between Stefan and me. His cheeks were red with rage or embarrassment, I couldn't quite tell. Either way, I was out of there. Grabbing the stroller, I spun it around, perching Angel on my hip and storming away from them before they could see my tears. They burned something fierce, but I refused to let them fall.

How could he be getting married? Married! *And* he had a role in a show. It was so damn unfair.

"Jody! JODY!" His terse voice chased me around the corner, but I kept walking. Angel was fussing in my arms, but I didn't want to slow down and strap her back into the stroller.

I squeezed her tightly against me, which only made her complaints louder.

"Jody, stop!" Stefan grabbed my arm, forcing me to stand beside him.

Not wanting to look him in the eye, I busied myself settling Angel back into the stroller and giving her a rattle to play with.

"How could you do that to me?"

"Do what? Tell your fiancée the truth? I was probably doing you a favor."

"That was *my* business!"

"No!" I slapped his hand off me. "It's ours. She's your daughter, Stefan!"

"I never wanted her. I told you that. It's not fair for you to punish me because you made a poor decision." His voice was strained, the tendons in his neck pulling tight.

"Excuse me?"

"You could have had this, Jody. You could have been performing by my side if you hadn't decided to keep the baby."

"Look at her!" I pointed into the stroller. "How could I possibly give her away?"

"I don't want to look at her." He kept his eyes on me, his face cresting with sadness. Thank God he hadn't whipped off those aviators yet. One glimpse of those chocolate orbs and my mind would turn into a puddly mess, especially when his voice dropped to a soft whisper. "I wanted you to come back. That was the plan, remember?"

His confession caught me off-guard, scorching

like hot fire.

"You didn't love me."

"I told you I did."

My voice was a squeak when I finally spoke. "But you didn't act like it. You never called me. You never checked in once."

"Look, I was mad at you, okay? I waited all summer, and then you never showed up for class. I couldn't exactly ask around, but the rumors told me enough. Jody, how could you?" He lightly touched my cheek, a fleeting caress that made my traitorous knees wobble. "You have so much talent, and you just threw it all away. How could you make a choice like that?"

He may as well have slapped me across the face.

I jerked away from the question, my eyes darting to the sidewalk as love and rage fought for dominance within me. He was trying to make *me* feel guilty? Like it was somehow *my* fault that things hadn't worked out between us!

Rage was winning. Thank God!

Clenching my jaw, I finally muttered, "I never chose for you to turn your back on me."

Stefan pulled off his shades, those brown eyes getting right in my face. Damn it!

"Don't put this on me." He snatched my arm, all charm vanishing from his voice. "Don't make me feel guilty. You had an out and you didn't take it."

"Let go of me." I tried to wriggle my arm free, but he held tight.

Angel's fussing had turned into full-blown wailing while I argued with her father. Her cheeks had turned red, but I ignored her cries, unable to look away from Stefan's mottled expression. His usually warm eyes were a dark cocoa. I didn't recognize them, and it made it so much easier to glare at him.

"And now you're trying to punish me by fucking up my relationship with Selene!"

"Let me go." My voice was rigid but still lacked the punch I really needed. His gripping fingers were actually starting to hurt. Desperation rippled through me, which hardly helped me get my Morgan on. I tried anyway, but my stupid voice wobbled over the words. "I mean it, Stefan, let me go."

"I think you should do as she says."

Stefan jumped at the sharp Australian voice behind him. He glanced over his shoulder, caught one glimpse of Leo's thunderous expression and dropped my arm immediately, taking a step back.

"Now piss off." Leo got in his face, stretching to his full height. He was still shorter than Stefan when he did that, but his attitude was ten times bigger. If this turned physical, I'd be putting my money on Leo for sure.

Stefan glared him down, but my boss was unperturbed. His arm muscles rippled as his fingers bunched into a fist. A tendon in Stefan's neck pinged tight, his eyes quickly calculating the threat in front of him. Finally, he backed off, throwing me a dark glare before sliding on his shades and stalking off in his pointy black shoes.

I couldn't move.

Angel's cries were a dull muffle in my ear. I knew I had to turn and collect her up, but I couldn't make myself do it.

"You all right?" Leo touched my arm.

I didn't respond.

Nudging me gently out of the way, he unbuckled Angel and lifted her into his arms.

"It's okay, cherry blossom." He nestled her against him, taking the stroller with his other hand. "Come on, let's walk your mum down to the beach and buy her a coffee, aye? You think she'd like that?"

His soft tone soothed Angel instantly, and she started her friendly face-slapping routine. Leo chuckled, letting her explore his whiskers and dip her tiny index finger into his barely there dimple.

I followed behind them, still feeling numb, hating myself for falling apart.

Hating myself for wishing that Stefan had pulled me into his arms, kissed away my tears, and told me he'd been a fool to ever let me walk away.

SEVENTEEN

JODY

Leo bought me a latte, and we strolled along the pier sipping quietly. Angel fell asleep a short while into our walk, but Leo still hadn't asked me who that guy was. I reached the dregs of my coffee, wishing for a few more mouthfuls.

"Here, I'll throw it out for you."

With a weak smile, I handed Leo my cup and watched him jog over to the trash can. He came back with an easy grin, and the words just tumbled out of me.

"That was Angel's father."

"I thought as much." He gave me a sympathetic

smile.

I looked away from it, keeping my eyes on the ocean as we walked up the steep hill, away from the pier. He guided the stroller to the upper pathway and we ambled along the winding route.

"He didn't hurt your arm, did he?"

"No." I rubbed the spot and shook my head. "Thank you for getting him to leave me alone."

"I didn't like the way he was talking to ya." Leo's frown was sharp, his anger obviously still on simmer.

"I kind of outed him to his fiancée. He was pretty pissed. I don't think she knew about Angel."

"Well, that's his problem, not yours."

I shrugged. "I guess." Tears sprung onto my lashes before I could stop them.

For goodness' sake, Jody! Leo's going to think the only thing you're good at is crying!

"Hey." His voice was soft as his hand landed on my lower back, rubbing slow circles.

"I'm sorry, it just feels so unfair some days. He's living the life I was supposed to have. He's in a show and it might go to Broadway and that's what *I* was training for." I slashed at my tears. "He told me I could make it and I believed him, because he was right." I stopped and leaned against the fence. "I could have made it, Leo. All my teachers said so...and I let them all down. You should have seen their faces when I admitted I was pregnant. Having to move back home and give it all up." I shook my head, fresh tears breaking free. "The thing that kills me now is that I made this huge decision to keep her, probably on impulse, because that's what I do and it felt right at the time, but seeing Stefan and what he's doing, I can't help questioning myself. I was confident in my old life, and now I'm totally floundering. I'm a terrible mother who yells at her child, gets in fights with her father, and ignores her crying. And I'm a useless housekeeper," I whined, not even caring that I sounded like a six-year-old.

"Hey, don't say that." He put the brakes on the stroller and leaned against the fence beside me, his arm pressing into mine. "Your house might be a little messy." He cleared his throat, a smile playing with the edge of his mouth. "But, Jo, you are a wonderful mum. You love your daughter. That's half the battle won right there."

"I can't help feeling like she deserves better some days. I don't know what I'm doing."

"Yes, you do. You are talented in more than just singing. You were born for more than a stage. This life you're living now is proving that. Leaving wherever you were and branching out on your own, that took courage."

A smile flittered across my face.

"And you're not failing. Angel is a happy, gorgeous girl who is being fed, watered, and loved." His hand ran down my back again. I liked the feel of it, that soft pressure that reminded me I wasn't alone. "I know it's not what you had planned, but this is a phase. Angel will grow, and you'll get your shot at the stage."

"Yeah, right." It was impossible not to be sarcastic. *Like I would ever make it now.* I'd missed my chance, sealed my fate when I locked myself into an eighteen-year parenthood plan.

He was nice enough not to reply to my swift shoot-down.

"I miss that life. The rehearsals, the buzz before a performance. That elation when people applaud you." My brow crinkled. "I miss him." I sucked in a ragged breath. "He was mad that I didn't come back, said I threw it all away."

"Yeah, I heard that part," Leo muttered.

"Do you think he's right?"

"No!" Leo looked incredulous as he jerked to face me. "If anyone's thrown anything away, it's him. What a bloody moron!"

My chuckle was dry. "A bloody handsome one. I hate that he's still so gorgeous. I hate that when I look at him, I want him to kiss me again and hold me and tell me that he made the biggest mistake of his life letting me go. Why does he have to be so beautiful, Leo?"

"He's not beautiful. Not in here." Leo tapped his heart. "At the end of the day, we're all going to be old and wrinkly. Looks are fleeting."

"Yeah. I guess."

"You don't want to be with a guy who turns his back on his own daughter. He didn't have to love you, but he should have been there. Any guy who turns his back on his kid..." Leo shook his head, a disgusted frown marring his features. "Ugly heart."

He stilled, his eyes bulging as he touched my arm. "I have the perfect song for this moment."

I couldn't help a cynical smile. He laughed at me as he pulled out his iPhone and unwound the earplugs around it.

"Pop this in." He handed me one and I put it in my right ear, while he shoved his into his left. I watched him open up Spotify. "Close your eyes, you really need to listen to these lyrics."

I did as I was told, smiling as the cheerful guitar rift started in my ear. I knew this song. "Ugly Heart" by G.R.L. My smile faltered as the lyrics began, speaking the words I needed to hear. I could feel my expression pinching as my emotions warred with the happy music versus the lyrics that wanted to eat at my soul.

Stefan was pretty, but Leo was right; he did have an ugly heart. As the second verse started talking about the guy getting married, my eyes flew open, and I caught Leo's gaze on me. I forced a smile, my chest still feeling tight and suffocating.

The second chorus kicked in, and it was near impossible to keep my hips still. My body moved of its own accord, and I had to clamp my lips together to keep from singing along. I didn't want to be dancing and singing. This song was painful to listen to, but it also made me feel better in a weird kind of way.

The slow chorus kicked in, and I felt the sadness sweep through me. I hadn't wanted to lose my virginity to a guy like that, but I had. I'd practically thrown it at him and I couldn't change it.

And I'd been wasting all these tears on him, pining for him, missing him when the truth had been staring me in the face.

I looked at Leo with my crestfallen expression as the singer's voice dipped away and then my boss totally surprised me. Leaning back with his eyes squeezed tight, he opened his mouth and hollered the line, "An ugly heart," with enough gusto to scare the people behind us. His arms flayed dramatically as he stayed with the line, leaning forward like a total pop star.

Giggles erupted from me before I could stop them. He looked hilarious.

"Sing it with me, Jo!" he shouted.

I laughed, standing tall and belting out the rest of the chorus, taking the top line and releasing the tension within me on those powerful notes. The song came to an abrupt end and by some miracle, Angel was still asleep.

Leo grinned at me, touching my shoulder lightly.

"You feel better?"

"Yeah." My smile was so broad it actually hurt. I didn't know what it was about this Australian man, but no one else had made me laugh this hard and smile this big since...I couldn't even remember when. "Let's listen to it again."

"Alrighty then." He pressed play and we swayed our hips, singing along to the entire song. His voice wasn't bad. Not Broadway good but still a nice, rich sound that was pleasant. My spirits lifted as I sang, feeling the words and aiming each one of them at Stefan. It felt good to let him go somehow, like a coil releasing inside of me and flooding my body with a sweet perfume.

I didn't think there'd ever be the right words to tell Leo how truly grateful I was.

He had been exactly what I needed in that moment.

EIGHTEEN

LEO

Seeing Jody go from tears to laughter had been pretty triumphant. I couldn't stop smiling. We'd strolled back to the apartment together, "Ugly Heart" leading into a bunch of other songs I had in that playlist. She'd started teasing me about my girly music collection.

"Hey, it's from my niece. She sends me her faves each week, and the list just keeps on growing."

"I love Spotify." She'd grinned.

Yet another thing to like about her.

I frowned, walking to the stereo and pumping up the volume on "Go" by Boys Like Girls. I was a little addicted to 'follow your dreams' type music. It kept me focused, kept reminding me why I'd broken my mother's heart and flown all the way over here. I had to keep my eye on Broadway.

I couldn't let one afternoon with a blonde beauty, eyes like the sky on a perfect day, stop me from following where I had to go.

Stepping into the kitchen, I hitched up my sweats, still too hot after my scalding shower to put on a shirt. I didn't know what to do with my evening. Part of me felt like composing, but I knew if I overdid that it'd end up hampering my creative flow, which was why I'd forced myself out for a walk earlier in the day and thank God I had. I'd wanted to rip that guy's arm off, the way he was towering over Jody like that, ignoring Angel's crying.

What a dickhead.

I hated the idea that he'd been with Jody. I could tell by his smarmy expression as he skulked away that he was all about the charm. He'd probably wooed Jody in with a few smiles, and she'd been putty in his hands.

Gripping the edge of the sink, I sucked in a calming breath and poured myself a glass of water, chugging it back.

"Now what are you going to do?" I wiped my bottom lip and gazed around the empty apartment, missing Gerry for a fleeting minute. I didn't know why. Our marriage had been cold and detached. I felt just as lonely the day I left as I had over the two years we were married, but still...it'd been a presence in the house.

"Maybe I should get a dog."

A rap at the door made me turn. Wiping my hands on my pants, I walked to the door and swung it open without bothering to check the peephole.

"Oh, hey." My smile was way too big. I tried to tone it down but couldn't quite do it.

Jody was standing there in the cutest PJ pants I'd ever seen. They had cartoon foxes all over them and a drawstring my fingers were itching to pull.

I pinched the door, taken aback by my thoughts. Where the hell had they come from?

Her cheeks were a little pink as she licked her lower lip. She seemed awkward, which I found strange after the easy-going day we'd shared.

Pushing a plate of cookies toward me, she cleared her throat and bobbed on her bare toes. Purple nail polish. Nice.

"I baked these for you, to say thanks."

"For what?" I took them, trying not to cringe when I noticed how burnt they were around the edges.

"Making me feel better today. Giving me that song."

"I'm glad it worked." There it was again, that puff of triumphant pride. I loved the idea that I was responsible for making her feel better. "Music always does the trick. I didn't want you wasting any more angst on a FIGJAM like that."

"Fig jam?" Her nose wrinkled, her ponytail resting on her shoulder as she tipped her head.

"You don't know that expression?"

She shook her head, her blue eyes dancing with anticipation.

I grinned, scratching the back of my neck. "It means, ah, Fuck I'm Good Just Ask Me."

That melodic giggle of hers sprung free, dancing all over me before it was cut short by her crumpling expression. "Oh my gosh, Stefan is such a FIGJAM!"

"Yep, total arrogant shithead." My voice grew sharp and snappy, making Jody's eyebrow quirk. She pressed her lips together, fighting a smile. I cleared the venom from my throat and muttered, "'Ugly Heart' could be his theme song."

Her smile grew as she nodded. "Your mom's right, you know. You do have a song for everything."

"I try to." Damn. I was blushing; I could feel it. I tried to pretend I wasn't, but I couldn't believe she'd remembered me saying that. "Music and lyrics can teach us so much about life and love. I like to let music guide me."

Jody's blue gaze grew warm, her lips curling with a grin. "Let music guide your love," she murmured. "I like that."

I captured the words, letting them dance through my brain, my smile growing in time with my nod. I had to write that down!

Jody crossed her arms, pushing her breasts up without even realizing it. The shoestring tank top that accompanied her PJ pants was powder blue and doing things to my body that were kind of out of my control. I hoped her gaze stayed north, because this would be bloody impossible to hide when going commando in sweatpants.

Thankfully her eyes stayed on my face, her top teeth lightly brushing over her lower lip.

Geez, I was going to have to slam the door in her face in a minute.

Pull it together, Leo!

Jody's head dipped, her high ponytail dropping over her shoulder. "You don't have to tell me, but have you ever had your heart broken before?" Her cheeks flushed. "I probably shouldn't even be asking you, but I keep thinking about today, and you were just so sympathetic and sweet and I just..." Her shoulders rose. "I couldn't help wondering."

Not loving the line of questioning, but appreciating the deflating effect it was having on my body, I decided to answer her. "Yeah, I was...married."

Her eyebrows shot up. "Wow, okay."

"Never really wanted to, but..." I rubbed my fingers through the stubble on my chin. "That's partly why I came over here. I just needed to get away from everything. I signed those divorce papers and felt like such a loser, so I decided I needed to figure out what I really wanted."

"So, you didn't want to get married, but you did anyway?"

I sighed. "I did say I was a loser."

Her lips pursed, her left shoulder hitching. "Sometimes it's hard not to give in to the pressure around you. It takes courage to stand up and fight for what you really want."

"I just hate that I dragged her down with me."

Jody nodded, giving me a sweet smile.

"So, what do you really want?"

I hesitated for only a second. If anyone was going to understand this dream, it'd be her. "I'm writing a musical to sell to Broadway."

Her eyes began to sparkle like fairy lights. "That is so cool."

"Thanks."

"Can I hear it?"

"Ah, no." I chuckled.

Her lip popped into a pout.

"Not until I'm finished."

"Okay." She nodded.

I wasn't quite sure what to say to her then. My throat had kind of swelled up with the idea of having to confess that she was my muse. I was worried if she heard any of the songs, saw me playing them for her, that she'd know in a heartbeat.

Her lips flirted with a shy grin before breaking past the emotion. She crossed her arms again, and I had to hold in my groan.

"Well, not to sound like a totally selfish bitch, but I'm kind of glad you understand that feeling of loss and heartache. I really appreciated that you got it today. You've never judged me or made me feel like an idiot for keeping Angel, and I know cookies and a thank you will never be enough."

I grinned, lifting the plate in my hand. "It's

enough, Jo."

"I hope you make it...to Broadway."

"Me too," I whispered, her sweet sentiment scratching at the edges of my heart.

Our gazes met, an intense connection that I could tell unnerved us both.

Jody stepped back from my door. "Okay, well, have a good night."

"You too." I tried to keep my gaze on her face, but my eyes just had to travel down her fine form one last time.

My body responded instantly. Thank God she turned away, because when I looked down I wasn't hiding anything. You could bloody camp out underneath that tent!

Rolling my eyes, I closed the door and headed back to the stereo, cranking it up one more notch and reminding myself why I'd come to America in the first place.

"New York, mate. Stay focused!"

NINETEEN

JODY

Leo smiling.

Leo's green eyes.

Leo's accent.

Leo! Leo! Leo! How was it possible to go from total nonchalance to taking him to bed with me in my dreams every night?

Leo shirtless. Not to sound shallow, but that's what did it.

Holy pectorals, the guy was ripped and he didn't even know it, just stood there casually holding the door like it was no big deal. Stefan was always so aware of how good-looking he was; Leo seemed oblivious. It took all my willpower not to stare blatantly at that fine cut torso and start drooling.

It wasn't just the shirtless-ness. I folded my arms tightly over my chest and forced myself to think about it. It was everything. It was the songs, it was the way his hand felt on my back when he comforted me, the way he threw my coffee cup away, the way he belted out those lyrics in an effort to make me laugh...the way he told Stefan to piss off and the way he stood up for me against the Cray-Cray.

It was all those little things that had taken him from Leo the *nice but weird Aussie* guy to Leo the *I think I might be falling in love with you* guy.

I squeezed my eyes shut. It was too fast, too sudden.

It was freaking insane!

"Jody, are you even listening?" Morgan's voice was sharp staccato in my ears. My eyes popped open obediently and I leaned forward in my chair.

"Uh-huh," I lied. "I was just closing my eyes to try and think of some more ideas."

Out of the corner of my eye, I saw Ella bite her lips together, burying her nose in Angel's hair to hide her smile.

Okay, so she didn't believe me. At least she couldn't read my mind! She already thought my neighbor was cute. The last thing I wanted to do was encourage my romantic bestie. If she could have her way, everyone in the world would be in love like her and Cole.

This couldn't be happening to me. I was still getting over Stefan. Okay, so I was basically *over* Stefan, and not even three beats later I'm pining for Leo?

Yeah, that's right, *pining*! Because the guy pretty much shut down after my cookie delivery, which meant I either sucked at baking or I should never have asked him about his broken heart.

I was such an idiot!

"So, what ideas have you had?" Morgan's pen tapped on her notepad.

I didn't know why she was so nervous about planning Sean's twenty-fifth birthday party. She was the organizational queen, but she'd been a total stress bucket over this thing.

"Um, dancing. We should definitely have that."

"It's already on the list," she snapped, turning back to Ella who was actually being helpful. "All we have to do now is finalize the food and beverages. Ella, make sure you guys keep a record of everything you give out at the bar so we can pay you back."

As soon as her eyes were off me, my mind wandered back to Leo. So what was with him? I mean, I knew he was busy. I heard the piano every time I walked out my door. He was working his caboose off composing this musical of his.

Maybe he was just distracted.

Or maybe he thought I was coming on to him!

I held in my groan.

Kill me now!

"Jody, seriously, what is your problem today?"

Morgan's brown eyes always grew darker when she was annoyed.

"Nothing." I shook my head, wishing I didn't feel so small beside her sometimes. Not that I was a pipsqueak like Ella, but Morgan was seriously tall for a girl and with her personality, it made her a force to be reckoned with.

Her hard edge vanished as her head tipped to the side. "Is everything okay at work?"

"Yeah, it's great." I bobbed my head, so relieved that I'd finished cleaning the house when she'd popped over the week before. Two hours earlier and she would have been shipping me back home or trying to move in with me.

I couldn't do that to her. She'd only just moved in with Sean. I didn't think he'd forgive her if she did the old change-a-roo on him. He was a nice, patient guy, but every man had his limits. Surely.

"Well, what's bothering you?"

"Nothing." My eyebrows were raised so high I thought they might jump into my hairline.

I grinned at Morgan's narrowed gaze, and thank goodness Angel started fussing. It was the perfect distraction. Ella passed her over. I nestled her against me, patting her back.

"You're tired, aren't you? Ready for a nap, huh?" I kept my voice soft and sweet. She nuzzled into my neck and I looked to Morgan. "I'm going to have to go soon. There's no way she'll fall asleep with us jabbering. Not unless I start walking."

"That's cool." Morgan got that mushy look on her face as she leaned forward and stroked the back of Angel's head. "Have you managed to find a babysitter for the party yet?"

"No." I frowned, laying Angel down in her stroller and adjusting the back so she was lying flat.

"Jody, why not? The party's this weekend."

"I know that. It's not like I haven't been trying, but Grandma Deb's off on the charity tour thing."

"So ask Dad."

"No way." I threw her a sharp frown. "He hasn't even been to the apartment yet. I've been living there for over two months now. We've said like five words to each other since the day I moved out. He hates me."

"He doesn't hate you."

"He thinks I'm screwing up again. He's mad at me."

"He's not mad, he's hurting. You kind of cut him off at the knees. He's waiting for you to make the next move."

Of course Morgan was standing up for him. It'd always been that way. Morgan was Dad's kid—same brown eyes, same outlook on life—but me...I was just like my mother.

Fear skittered through me at the very idea. I busied myself arranging Angel's blanket, making sure she was snug for the walk home.

Thankfully Morgan dropped it, but that still didn't solve my problem. Morgan would be gutted if I didn't come to Sean's party, but I couldn't take my baby into a bar with thumping music and rowdy partygoers.

"Why don't you ask Leo?" Ella's question was

soft and sweet, yet it still made me flinch.

"What?" Morgan spoke for me.

"Oh, come on, why not?" Ella shrugged, her big eyes innocent as she tucked a lock of mouse-brown hair behind her ear. "He lives just across the hall from you. You said he was great with Angel."

He was!

Another reason to love him.

I frowned.

"It's only one night. Angel will probably already be asleep by the time you leave, won't she?"

"Close to it." I nodded in spite of the fact I should have been shaking my head.

"So, if there's no one else, it's a viable option."

I caught Morgan's gaze on me and chose to ignore it. She'd only met Leo once and had already made up her mind about the guy before she spoke to him. Although, after some badgering from Ella, she did concede that he seemed nice enough for a boss. She was just annoyed with me for branching out on my own.

Or worried.

Whatever, she was being big sister Morgan.

I gripped the stroller handle and tried to think of a line to appease both of them. "I'll think about it."

I walked away before more could be said and sped home. Angel fell asleep within five minutes of leaving the cafe, so I put some buds in my ears and sang my way home. I was waiting for the elevator, quietly singing "How Sweet It Is" with Michael Buble when Leo appeared behind me. I saw the shadow out of the corner of my eye and nearly jumped a mile.

He chuckled. "Sorry about that."

"No problem." I turned down the music, trying to keep my cool.

"Great song. Buble does the best version."

"Yeah, I think so, too." I grinned. "I love his voice so much."

"He's the modern-day Frank."

"So true."

We smiled at each other, our gazes kissing then jumping to the floor.

The elevator doors dinged open, and we stepped in together. Leo peeked into the stroller, his smile softening as he looked down at my sleeping Angel.

The expression on his face was adorable!

"Hey, I don't suppose you're free to babysit on Saturday, are you?"

Jody, what the hell are you doing?

"Um, sure. I think so." Leo scratched the back of his neck. "You got a hot date or something?" His chuckle was hard and awkward.

"Ah, no." I snickered, finding the idea ludicrous. "It's my sister's boyfriend's birthday."

"Oh, he's that actor, right? The *Superstar* guy?"

"That's the one." I nodded. "She's planning a big party, and she really wants me to be there."

"Absolutely. I'll be happy to watch Angel for ya."

"Thank you." The elevator reached the top floor and Leo let me push the stroller out first.

"So, what time?"

"She's picking me up at seven. She's forcing me to help her set up."

Leo chuckled. "Siblings, aye?"

"Yeah." I grinned.

"See you on Saturday then."

"Okay." I fumbled my keys trying to get them in the lock, scolding myself for being excited about what would no doubt be a ten-minute encounter with the guy in a few nights' time.

I was so pathetic.

TWENTY

LEO

I tried not to think too hard about seeing Jody on Saturday night. I'd kind of taken the chicken's way out and avoided her since seeing her in her PJs. I'd only slept with one woman in my life, and she had never caught me off-guard like Jody did. I mean, Gerry had swooped me up pretty easily, but she'd really been trying. Jody hadn't done anything but pass me a plate of cookies. She hadn't been flirty and seemed completely unaware of her intoxicating power.

I never thought I'd find cute sexy. Gerry was a sophisticated woman, hair always perfect, make-up pristine. Jody was the polar opposite, and she had me waking most nights with tents for pants and bugger all I could do about it.

I couldn't make a move on her. The whole point of being in the States was to make my dreams come true, and settling down with a wife and kid did not fit into the plan.

I was an idiot to say yes to babysitting, but when I heard she wasn't out on some hot date, I'd been so relieved I had to agree.

Rapping twice on the door, I rocked back on my heels, waiting for Jody to appear.

"It's open!" she called.

I eased the handle and pushed the door wide, stepping in and surveying the living area. It looked pretty good. The dishes were drying in the rack, there was still a pile of unfolded laundry on the edge of the couch, but the house didn't have that chaotic feel.

"Sorry, I'm coming." Jody's voice wafted from the bedroom and a few seconds later she appeared.

Oh, geez, I really was an idiot.

There was absolutely nothing cute about the image before me. Jody looked frickin' hot, like flames on a barby...the kind you wanted to get burned with. She was wearing a deep red dress that plunged between her breasts and accentuated her curves, giving them a luscious, edible quality. The bottom skirt-part-thingy rose up over her knees and draped down lower at the back, swirling around her like water when she moved. She was wearing these strappy sandals that wove around her ankles and calves. They looked bloody uncomfortable, but who really cared. She'd taken *fine* to a whole new level.

Thank God I'd worn undies and jeans tonight. Hopefully the little general would stay on lockdown in the confined space.

Squirming in my pants, I tried to order the guy into submission while throwing a grin at Jody.

A whistle came out of my mouth as I nodded my appreciation. "You look amazing."

"You think so?" Her nose wrinkled, her head tipping to the side, and I spotted PJ girl again. There she was under all that make-up. The little cutie.

My pants got tighter and I cleared my throat, crossing my arms and trying to draw her eyes north. "So, um, any instructions for me?"

"Oh, um, not really. Angel's asleep already. She had a really short nap this afternoon, so was totally toasted." Jody clipped into the kitchen. "If she wakes, just give her a bottle." She opened up the pantry and showed me where everything was. "Feel free to help yourself to anything. Sorry, I haven't had a chance to do any baking."

"No problem." I choked out the words, hoping she'd never find out I'd thrown her cookie-rocks away.

She smiled at me, her dark red lips familiar yet so incredibly different. It fascinated me that she could appear as two such distinct women. She scratched the side of her nose, a blush forming beneath her make-up.

Actually, not that distinct. She was still my Jo. Assistant, my *assistant*, Jo.

A knock sounded at the door, saving my life. Jody answered it quickly, and I waved at Morgan as her head popped into view.

"Hey, Leo." She was still reserved with me, but at least her sharp face was smiling this time.

"Nice to see you, Morgan."

"Mm-hm." Her perfectly shaped eyebrows rose.

Jody flicked her a frown before turning to me, a sunshine smile beaming from her face. "Thank you so much for doing this. I'll have my phone on me the whole night, so just call me if anything goes wrong."

"It won't. Everything's going to be fine, trust me."

"Yeah, but if she wakes and she's upset. I mean, I told her you were coming, but she's only like eleven months old so I didn't, I wasn't sure—"

"Jo, just go and have a good time."

"Yeah, okay." She gave me a sheepish grin, her eyes lingering on me for a minute.

I cut the contact, looking to the floor with an awkward swallow. I glanced back up in time to see her cheeks flame red, a scorching look of disappointment cresting over her face.

What was that about?

"See ya," she mumbled, shutting the door behind her.

I didn't have time to decipher more. I stared at the door for a few minutes, my body frozen as I tried to talk myself out of feeling this way. Jody didn't need me roping her in and then ditching her. If an opportunity came up in New York, I knew I'd have to take it. The best thing I could do for her was to keep things platonic.

Besides, Jody wouldn't be interested in some divorcé. She needed a stable guy with a good, stable job who could take care of her.

"Like she'd be interested in you anyway, mate." I flopped onto the couch, my head landing on the pile of unfolded laundry. Sitting up with a sigh, I grabbed the wrinkled T-shirt off the top and began folding.

I'd gotten a fair assessment of Stefan. He was nothing like me—clean-cut, refined, sophisticated. He belonged on a Milan catwalk. Shaggy old me was probably the last thing Jody was interested in.

I laid the folded shirt on the floor and rubbed at my whiskers. Maybe I should be shaving more.

"Shut the hell up, you big dick." I snatched a bright pink baby shirt off the pile, grinning at its cuteness before attempting to fold it. "You just bloody said you don't want to rope her in!" I muttered to myself. "New York. New York. New York." The words came out in soft whispers until my singing voice kicked in and the lyrics for "Empire State Of Mind" flowed out of me.

The music soothed me, reminding me of everything I was working toward. I couldn't let cute little pink T-shirts and a sexy mama stop me from striving for that.

TWENTY-ONE

JODY

"He called you Jo," Morgan said as soon as we hopped into her car.

"Huh?" I buckled up, refusing to look at her. I didn't want her to see my searing disappointment. Leo so wasn't interested in me. I mean, yeah, he thought I looked pretty tonight, but even if he did like me, he wasn't after anything. He had bigger dreams to pursue. I'd been a total fool to even let myself daydream.

"No one ever calls you Jo." Morgan pulled away from the curb.

I shrugged. "He does."

"You like it, don't you?"

I sighed, leaning my head back and totally forgetting it was pinned up. I winced and moved forward again, fingering the do and hoping I hadn't dislodged any pins.

"I like that he calls me something different. It's nice to be in a completely different world. He doesn't look at me as though I'm screwing up my life. He treats me with respect."

Morgan changed gears, her expression folding as if she was about to cry.

I touched her arm. "Hey, what's wrong? What did I say?"

She shook her head and slowed for the red light, turning to me once we'd stopped completely. "I'm sorry if I ever made you feel like a screw-up. You're not, Jody. You've done so well with Angel and getting a job. You've set yourself up great, and you're going to be just fine."

"Thanks." I forced a tight smile, feeling like none of it was true.

Okay, so it was partially true. Over the last couple of weeks I had felt slightly more in control. I was staying on top of my job and mostly parenthood, but setting myself up? For what? The future still seemed pretty bleak to me. The idea of maintaining an apartment building while raising a child on my own hardly thrilled me. I could feel the lingering depression creeping into my psyche again. I didn't want it to win. I'd been feeling good lately. I didn't want to dip back down again.

I pressed my lips together, forcing light

conversation about the party. Morgan was all organized, feeling a jittery excitement. It was actually a surprise party for Sean, which I'd only just realized. Thank goodness I hadn't seen him lately. I totally would have spilled the beans! No wonder she'd been nervous.

All Sean knew was that Morgan was taking him out for the night to celebrate his birthday. He was to meet her at Reynolds for a quick drink then go from there. What he didn't know was that waiting at the bar were all his closest friends and a few of his family.

Morgan had gone out of her way to make sure everyone knew (except clueless me!) that it was a surprise thing. She didn't want the paparazzi showing up.

"Some of the *Superstar* cast are going to be there, so I really hope they've kept their mouths shut."

"Is Travis coming?" I winked at my sister, giggling when she threw me an incredulous look. Travis had been her super-evil boss when she worked on set with Sean, and he'd nearly broken Morgan, something I never thought anyone could do. Thankfully she'd quit, and then Sean had put him in his place. Man, I wish she'd recorded that jackass's apology. I would have *loved* to hear it.

We parked behind the building, next to Cole and Ella's car. They'd reserved a spot for us. I jumped out and moved the cone then followed Morgan in the back entrance once she'd locked up. The kitchen smelled amazing. Cole and Ella's staff was working tonight, catering the event, and Ella had actually managed to persuade Cole out from behind the bar for once.

I knew he would struggle with it. Reynolds was his baby.

Ella wrapped me in a hug and gushed about how beautiful we both were. She looked pretty damn hot herself in a black leather skirt and fitted red blouse, something made all too obvious by the fire in Cole's eyes every time he glanced at her.

Those two.

I shook my head with a grin.

We spent an hour finishing off decorations and then people started filtering in. I was put on meet-and-greet, forcing plastic smiles to a bunch of people I only kind of knew. I used to be great at this role, but I just didn't feel like it tonight. It sucked watching all these couples swan in, holding hands, laughing together as they handed me their coats and jackets.

Ella and I dutifully put them away while Morgan roamed the room.

"He's coming!" Sean's sister squealed from the door.

We took cover, crouching behind tables while Morgan dimmed the lights. A few seconds later, the door creaked open and Sean called into the darkened space, "Hello?"

We all jumped up with a roar, and as the lights went up we started singing "Happy Birthday." Sean ran a hand over his buzz cut, looking sheepish as he grabbed Morgan to his side, grinning down at her before dipping her for a long-winded smooch.

Everyone burst into laughter and cheered him on.

"Thank you, everyone!" He raised his hand, enjoying the applause, although still a little embarrassed by the surprise. His large hand splayed over Morgan's side, and he murmured something into her ear. She giggled, her cheeks blushing pink before he kissed her again. I couldn't take my eyes off them. Sean's dark skin pressed against Morgan's milky-white complexion was always so beautiful to me. They were like dark cocoa and white chocolate.

Cole got some music pumping. I was surprised there wasn't a live band. Reynolds was famous for their live shows.

"We tried to get Chaos, but they had to cancel last-minute. Jimmy's got the flu." Ella looked sad.

"Aw, man, that would have been awesome."

"I know, but he has to get better pronto. They've made the semi-finals for the show."

"What show?" Great, more people making their dreams come true. Lucky them!

"Oh, did you not hear? They got accepted for *Shock Wave*. It's kind of like a reality show, competition thing."

"You mean like *American Idol*?"

"Kind of." She nodded. "But for bands instead. The winners get a recording contract with Torrence Records—full album and a tour."

"No way!" My enthusiasm was forced; I could feel it.

"Cool, right? Troy's super-excited to have his baby brother in LA for filming."

"Who's Troy again?"

"Cole's friend from high school. I thought you'd met him?"

I shook my head, my lower lip popping out.

"Well, I'll have to arrange a big dinner or something, so you can meet everybody. I'll make sure Chaos comes, as well."

"Sounds good." My smile became genuine, fueled by my best friend's excited grin.

Ella and Cole had a very special connection to Chaos. Not only was Cole buddies with the lead singer's brother, but they were the band that accompanied Cole when he serenaded Ella off her feet and straight into his arms.

It was the most romantic, swoon-worthy story ever. Singing in public to the one you love? It doesn't get better than that. You know someone loves you when they do that kind of thing.

I crossed my arms, trying hard not to think about how loveless my life had become. Stefan may have sung for me, but only in private.

Leo had sung for me in public...but he didn't want me.

Ella pulled me onto the dance floor, which was a total blessing, because I was on the verge of sinking into a puddle of tears in the corner. I forced my happy on, getting caught up in the dance music thumping through the bar.

About an hour or so into it, the music came to a halting stop and Sean called everyone's attention. Cole handed him a mic while Morgan came to stand beside me against the bar.

"Hey, everyone. I just want to say thanks again for throwing this party for me. I feel very loved right now." Everyone awwed and he batted his hand in the air, silently telling us to shut up. "I want to say a special thank you to my oh-so-fine woman, who I love more than anyone in the world."

I squeezed Morgan's arm, feeling all warm and gooey for her. Ella jumped in next to her, an adorable smile on her face. I grinned then flicked my eyes back to Sean, who was also wearing the sweetest look I'd ever seen. His eyes sparkled as he gazed at Morgan, and a song started playing through the loudspeaker. I gasped, recognizing the tune, and then Sean started singing "Marry Me" by Jason Derulo. I swear every girl in the room teared up instantly.

Morgan went rigid beside me, her eyes bulging wide.

"Oh my gosh!" Ella squeezed Morgan's arm.

I glanced from my sister back to the stage area. Sean was getting into the song, sounding *amazing* as he danced and swayed to the thumping beat.

Morgan folded her arms. "This is so embarrassing. How can he ask me in front of all these people?"

"Well, he's asked you in private and you keep saying no. He's obviously trying new tactics."

Morgan's lips twitched. "I'm gonna kill him."

My snicker was dry as I nudged her with my elbow. "And then what are you gonna do?"

"Say yes." She looked straight at me, a smile

taking over her face as she stepped toward the stage.

Sean grinned, dropping to his knees and sliding across the floor, finishing the move with a little spin that stopped right at Morgan's feet. The song was still playing, Sean still singing when he dipped into his pocket and pulled out a black box.

My chest restricted, a combination of sheer joy for my sister and utter desolation for me.

I was the one with the kid. Shouldn't I have been the one getting married?

The song came to an end. Sean slipped the ring on Morgan's fourth finger, and she bent down to kiss him. The entire room erupted with applause, Sean and Morgan chuckling against each other's lips as he rose from the floor.

I'd never seen her look so happy.

This was it. She was making a family of her own now and she deserved it.

Cole approached, wrapping his arm around Ella and whispering something in her ear. Her cheeks flushed pink and he laughed, kissing the top of her head. They gazed at each other adoringly. I knew what they'd be doing later.

What would I be doing?

I'd be going home to a cold, lonely bed to be woken at sparrow's fart by a crying baby, who yes, I loved dearly, but...

With a grimace, I slapped the bar, grabbing the bartender's attention. I ordered a straight vodka shot. He gave it to me without even hesitating, handing it over with a smile. I gulped it down and ordered a second one. If I had to stay at this party surrounded by all these loved-up couples who were getting married and seeing all their dreams come true, the least I could do was dull my awareness of them.

TWENTY-TWO

LEO

It was getting close to midnight and Jody still wasn't home. I shouldn't have really been surprised. Midnight was hardly a late night out, but I was getting tired, and I wasn't sure how Jody would feel about me falling asleep on her couch.

Angel had woken at ten, crying like a banshee. She was not impressed to find her mother missing, but I'd fed her a bottle, following the instructions on the formula tin to the letter. She'd guzzled it down and fallen asleep in my arms.

It was impossible not to feel totally protective of her as I walked her back to bed and laid her down.

She stirred, her face puckering with an incoming wail, so I sang her a lullaby, "Jesus Loves Me." Mum had sung it to all us kids when we were growing up, and I'd heard my sister-in-law, Deb, singing it to her little sprats, too. They all seemed to like it.

Angel settled down with a soft sigh, and I crept out of the room, my heart squeezing tight. Was it possible to fall in love with a kid you weren't even related to?

I was just drifting to sleep with that question blurring through my head when I heard a sound in the corridor outside. I jerked upright and leapt over the couch, opening the door to the tall, dark-haired guy who'd helped Jody move in a couple of months back.

He was carrying Jody in his arms. She was a floppy mess.

My eyes bulged wide as he greeted me, reminding me who he was. "What happened?"

"Vodka shots." Cole winced. "And before you ask, yes, I'm firing my bartender." Cole leaned forward, obviously intending to pass Jody to me. "She fell asleep in the car. Are you good to carry her to bed? Ella's holding down the fort on her own, and I'd really like to get back as quick as I can."

"Yeah, yeah, of course, mate." I took her in my arms.

She smelled pretty bad, but alcohol aside, she felt amazing.

Cole stroked a curl lightly off her face. "I don't

know what got into her tonight and why we didn't notice." He looked annoyed with himself.

"She'll be right." I gave him a reassuring smile. "I'll look after her."

"Thanks." His smile was broad and sincere as he headed for the elevator. "Ella will no doubt come by to check on her tomorrow."

"Good." I nodded, hitching Jody into my arms and swinging the door closed with my butt. The noise roused Jody. Her head jerked off my shoulder and she winced, her eyes fuzzy as they gazed around the room.

"Angel," she murmured.

"Tucked up safe in bed." I carried her toward her bedroom, figuring she could sleep in her dress. I'd need take her shoes off, though...if I could figure out how. I didn't want to turn the light on and hoped the beam from the hallway would be enough to help me wrestle through the task.

Jody's smile was soft and sweet as I laid her down. She cringed, tugging at some pins in her hair and struggling to pull them free.

"Here, let me." I sat down on the edge of the bed beside her and gently removed the pins, running my fingers through her thick locks of hair. Her head felt limp in my hands, and I laid it down on the soft pillow. "Thanks, Cole," she whispered, her eyes fluttering closed.

I grinned, moving to her feet to tackle the shoes. She must have been pissed if she couldn't differentiate my voice from Cole's.

"Morgan's getting married," she murmured.

My fingers went still on the tiny buckle of her right sandal.

The ache in her voice tugged at my heart. "Sean's proposal was...beautiful and I'm so happy for her." The wobbling voice and crestfallen expression told me otherwise. I quickly wrestled with the buckle of her shoe so she could curl up and go to sleep. No wonder she'd gotten drunk.

"Shouldn't I be the one getting married? I've got the kid!" Jody hiccupped. "And she's gonna...grow up without a dad, because..." She sucked in a ragged breath and squeaked, "He doesn't want us."

I managed to get the first shoe off, dropping it to the floor and getting to work on the other one. I kept my voice soft and soothing.

"Angel has men in her life who care about her, who will help you raise her. Uncle Cole, Uncle Sean..." I licked my bottom lip and whispered, "Uncle Leo."

"Oh, Leo." She sighed. "I love that guy."

I froze, her shoe clutched in my hand. "You what?"

"I love him." Her speech was slurred but still coherent enough to get my heart accelerating up my throat. "I don't just mean like...I love him, like...you'd love a friend, but I really...love him, you know!" Her voice rose. "Like, I've totally...fallen for him. It's insane, but I can't help it. He's just so...everything!" Her arms flopped up then crashed down onto the bed as her expression crumpled again.

I dropped the shoe and came around beside her, brushing the wayward curls off her face.

Her eyes popped open, and she looked straight at me, those blue orbs working their magic.

I couldn't breathe.

"You can't tell him," she whispered.

"Why n—?"

"Shhh!" She slapped her hand over my mouth, her eyes bulging wide. "He can never know."

I gently freed my lips, holding her hand and rubbing my thumb over her soft skin. "Why not?"

"I don't think...he wants me." She pouted.

I nearly opened my mouth to protest, but she saved my bacon and kept talking.

"Besides...even if he did...he's too talented. He's gonna sell his musical to Broadway, you know? And be amazing." Her voice became a whisper, like it was a floating wisp on the wind that she couldn't catch or control. "I'll just drag him down... hold him back. He deserves his dreams. I can't...take that away...from him. I've got a kid...and my—my dreams were shot to hell the day...I got pregnant. I've accepted that." She frowned. "Sort of." Licking her lower lip, she smacked them together and rolled to her side, mumbling, "He wants Broadway more than me...and that's the way...it should be."

Her sentence petered off to barely audible, but I was pretty sure I caught the last part. My heart ached as I moved off the bed and stumbled back to the couch in the living room. I wasn't leaving. Jody was totally plastered and might not even hear Angel if she woke.

Stretching out on the couch, I rested my ankles on the armrest and propped my hand behind my head, gazing up at the ceiling and trying to figure out the torrent of emotions surging through me.

Jody Pritchett loved me.

My lips rose into a half-smile before I could even stop them.

TWENTY-THREE

JODY

I was woken by the sound of a blender. I jerked up and then flopped back down with a groan, clutching my head and cursing myself. What the heck had I done the night before, and why did I feel like Satan was having a party in my head?

I sat up, taking in my red dress and half exposed boob. I heard laughter from the kitchen and quickly adjusted myself, wondering who the hell was in my house.

"Angel," I murmured, lurching to my feet and wanting to pass out from the swift movement.

I stumbled into the kitchen, nearly tripping over

my feet. A strong arm caught me, guiding me to one of the bar stools.

"You right?"

Aussie accent.

Leo.

Everything was okay.

I squinted, grinning sheepishly as the guy beside me chuckled.

"Well, you know for a sheila who came in completely trashed last night, I'd say you're not looking too bad."

Angel squealed in her high chair, obviously excited to see me. I winced at the loud sound but tipped forward and kissed her head, tasting banana and applesauce. Yep, it was feeding time at the zoo. "Hey, cupcake," I croaked.

She whacked her spoon against the plastic tray and kicked her legs, making a funny buzzing noise with her tongue.

Leo chuckled. "You're getting pretty good at that, aren't you, sloppy." He dashed a face cloth under her chin and placed her plastic sippy cup of water on the tray. She snatched it up and started guzzling.

As my eyes adjusted to the seriously strong light in the room, I started noticing how tidy my house was.

"Wow, I actually folded my laundry," I muttered. "I don't remember doing that."

I glanced at Leo who was fighting a grin for some reason.

"Do you remember much about last night?" He

took the lid off the blender and poured some thick, green goop into a glass.

I shook my head, instantly regretting the move. Nursing my temple, I groaned. "No. Fuzzy. Everything's fuzzy." I licked my parched lips, my tongue feeling fat and gummy in my arid mouth.

Leo smiled, setting the glass down in front of me and leaning back against the other counter. He crossed his arms, accentuating those luscious muscles of his. I tried not to notice.

"What's this?" I frowned at the concoction.

"It's called Kev and Leo's hangover cure." He laughed at my doubtful frown. "Trust me, it works every time."

My lips curled with disgust as I lifted the glass to my nose and gave it a sniff. I glanced up at him again. He gave me an encouraging nod, looking far too sexy in his fitted jeans and wrinkled T-shirt. I liked him standing in my kitchen, feeding my daughter and looking after me way too much for my own good.

I drew in a breath and pressed the glass to my mouth, slugging it back. It tasted foul, and I gagged twice trying to finish it. Leo passed me a glass of water, and I chugged that back, as well.

"Thatta girl." He clapped his hands. "I know it's pretty gross, but you'll be feeling better soon." He winked at me, taking the glass away and rinsing it in the sink.

Placing the glass upside down in the rack, he turned to me, wiping his hands on his jeans before heading to Angel's high chair and cleaning her up.

Once she was applesauce and banana free, he popped her down on the floor. She immediately dropped to her haunches and crawled over to the toy box, pulling out the bright pink doll and shoving the foot in her mouth.

I smiled softly, my head starting to clear just a little.

"She's like a cherub, isn't she?" Leo watched her, a slight look of awe enhancing his already gorgeous face.

"Yeah." I nodded, turning to him and losing myself in his tender expression.

He caught my gaze and cleared his throat, stepping back into the kitchen and wiping down Angel's messy tray. I couldn't speak while he worked; my eyes kept darting from my baby on the floor to the sex god in the kitchen.

My cheeks flushed pink as my mind began to wander to a place with no clothes and two hot bodies intertwined on a bed. Heat rushed through my core, and I jerked out of my stool, throwing him a shaky smile when he spun to face me.

Forget it, Jody. It's not going to happen!

No, my feelings for Leo had to remain a secret. He didn't need to know how gone I was for him. He had more important things to do with his life than stick around looking after me and a baby that wasn't even his.

"Listen, you should get going." I flicked my hand before pointing into the living room. "I'm just going to have a quiet day here, you should go...work...or whatever it is you do on a...ah..."

"Sunday."

"Sunday." I clicked my fingers and pointed at him.

"Okay." He nodded, pushing off the counter and heading to the door.

"Hey, Leo." I turned, my head still feeling sloshy, but better than when I first woke. "Thank you for sticking around this morning and helping me out."

"Of course. All part of the babysitting service." He winked.

"Oh, yeah." I flushed. "Here, I should pay you." I searched the counter for my wallet.

"Don't be insane." He waved his hand at me. "I was just helping out a neighbor last night. It was really no big deal."

He held the door in his hand, looking at me with a sweet sparkle in his eyes.

Holy hot lips, I wanted to kiss him so bad right now.

I pressed my lips together and forced a tight smile. "Well, thank you."

The door clicked shut behind him, and my day went downhill from there.

*****

Watching my "good neighbor" leave my apartment had sucked. About two minutes after he left, Angel started crying. I winced at the piercing sound, picking her up and trying to entertain her while I got rid of last night's stench. In the end I popped her in the shower with me, which was fine but hardly relaxing, especially when I accidentally got soap in her eye. Note to self, don't be scrubbing your body with a soapy loofah when your baby is sitting on the shower floor.

It took her way too long to get over that incident, and she ended up screaming her bloodshot eyes to sleep. I felt so terrible. Guilt played with me for the rest of the day, tormenting me in my sleep as I tried to recover from the previous night.

Ella woke me from a fitful nap to check up on me, and then Morgan called about a half hour later to tell me off for drinking too much. Her phone call woke Angel, so she didn't have long to chew my ear out. She did at least apologize for waking my baby and turning my afternoon into the longest one ever.

By the time I crawled to my bed, I felt like total shit but of course couldn't find the comfort of sleep.

I wanted Leo back in the house again. I wanted him in my bed, holding me as I slept. I wanted him to wake up beside me and suggest the perfect song to start the day with.

But he wasn't beside me. In fact that next day he wasn't even home, and the Cray-Cray was all up my ass with complaints about his kitchen faucet. He was forced to deal with me because Leo wasn't around, and after a day of insults, I needed Leo's song list more than anything.

I was tempted to pop over the next day and ask for a bunch of suggestions to get me through the crap-fest of a week I was having, but I forced myself not to. He wasn't my boyfriend. He was my boss, my neighbor, and that was it. I just had to accept it!

Angel kicked her legs and squealed. It wasn't the delightful one I enjoyed; it was the impatient, 'get me out of this high-chair' one.

"In a minute, baby. Just let me get these dishes done."

She started to cry, slamming her sippy cup on the plastic tray before throwing it on the floor.

"Angel!" I spun around with a scowl. "I'm asking for five minutes. Give me a break!" I wiped my forehead with my arm, managing to smear my cheek with dish suds. I groaned, snatching the towel off the counter.

Angel continued to cry.

"Not long," I sing-songed, putting on the sweetest voice I could muster.

She'd been clingy all day, and I knew the second I let her out of that high-chair, she'd want me to hold her. The dishes had been piling up all day, and I was running out of clean cutlery and plates. This was my only chance.

I scrubbed ferociously at a plate that had last night's food stuck to it. Lifting it out of the sudsy water, I checked it was clean before rinsing it quickly and smashing it into the rack. Angel's cries were increasing in volume, my nerves becoming a tattered mess with each new wail. Snatching up Angel's half-eaten plate of food, I spun to tell her I'd be done in a minute when it slipped from my fingers, landing on the floor with a smack and plastering my kitchen cupboards with spaghetti sauce.

"Shit!" I screeched, making Angel wail even louder. I rolled my eyes. "I'm sorry," I whined. "Just give me a sec to clean this up or you're going to crawl meat sauce all through this place."

She kicked her legs and slapped her hands on the tray in frustration. Closing my eyes, I kneaded my temples and dropped to my knees, snatching the cloth as I went. I didn't even know where to start. It looked like lasagna had puked all over my kitchen.

The day couldn't end fast enough!

A loud thumping noise from the outside corridor distracted me. I recognized the song immediately—the beat-clap, beat-clap of the opening rift always brought a smile to my face. "Dance With Me Tonight" by Olly Murs. I loved that song! My head popped up with a confused frown as the door clicked open and Leo slid into the room, a fedora tilted on his head. He did a spin as the announcer introduced Olly Murs, and then he started mouthing the words, walking toward Angel with a little skip.

Laughter rumbled in my tummy when Leo started doing a twist and shimmy as he sang a little Olly to my baby girl. Angel stopped crying immediately, enthralled by the performance. As the chorus kicked in, Leo reached down and unbuckled her, lifting her out of the chair and twirling her around. Her delighted giggles and squeals added to the music, and the smile on my face stretched so wide, my cheeks started hurting.

I watched Angel and Leo bop around the space between the door and the couch, Angel giggling so hard, her face was bright red. Leo caught my eye as the song kicked into the second chorus. He pointed his finger at me then twisted his hand, beckoning me over as he mouthed the words.

The cloth in my hand slapped onto the floor, spaghetti sauce be damned. I danced towards them, my hips twisting with the energetic beat. Laughter bubbled out of me as Leo caught me with his spare hand, spinning me around and bringing me back to his side. We bopped around as a little threesome, all three of us laughing and grinning like idiots.

It was the perfect song, turning my day completely on its head and making me fall just a little bit more in love.

TWENTY-FOUR

LEO

I sat at my piano, tinkering with an upbeat melody. I could picture a scene in a bland grey hall, no color, no joy, no light, and then the protagonist bursts onto the stage, a rainbow of sound and emotion, bringing the place to life with her jubilant energy.

I paused, grinning as I recaptured the moment in Jody's place a couple of hours earlier. When I'd first got out of the lift and heard Angel wailing, I'd cringed. I figured it was a bad moment. Jody was yelling something about being done in a minute and I took a risk.

A risk that had paid off. The look of light radiating from Jody, the sounds of Angel's laughter, combined into a perfect moment that had me falling further than I ever thought possible.

As soon as the song was done, Jody took Angel for a bath, and I cleaned up the kitchen for her. She didn't ask me to, but I figured it was the last thing she'd probably feel like after putting Angel to bed. I snuck out while she was still bathing her girl.

Part of me had wanted to stay, but it really wasn't my place.

Jody had told me she loved me, but she'd been drunk and thought she was talking to Cole. I couldn't make a move on her in good conscience. Besides, she'd been right. I did want New York, Broadway, my dream. The musical was nearing completion. I'd given the outlined proposal to Bobby a few weeks ago and was working my way through the orchestral arrangements. Bobby had started giving me recording time in one of the studios he part-owned, so I could get the tracks down on the piano and make them sound really good. One of the tech guys was giving me a hand with the digital stuff, teaching me things along the way. Because of him, I could turn my piano solo into a full-blown orchestral piece. I'd spent an entire day there during the week, preparing the backing track for the song I'd want to pitch if the proposal garnered a bit of interest. It sounded pretty damn good, and I was looking forward to doing more. I just needed to find the right singer to complete the track.

The phone in my pocket buzzed, and I answered it on the third ring.

"Hey, Bobby, how's it going?"

"Yeah, good, thanks, kid. Listen, I just wanted to let you know that I finally pinned down my guy in New York. He's taken your proposal, and he'll look it over this weekend."

"Awesome!" I shuffled in my seat, excitement skittering through me.

"He's not promising anything, but he'll look."

"No, that's fine, mate. I'll take whatever I can get."

"Good. There are a couple of hours free in the studio tomorrow if you want to do another recording session. Last-minute cancellation."

"Okay, put me down. I'll be there." My head bobbed like I was a cartoon character. "Thank you so much for this, Bobby."

"Not a problem, kid. Have a good night."

I hung up and pumped my fist in the air. "Yes!"

Mate, that felt good! I knew it could lead to nothing, but it could also lead to everything I wanted. I was tempted to jump up and do a happy dance.

A knock at the door made me pause. I knew who it was; I could tell by the way my heart jackknifed and skidded down to my stomach. With my already giddy excitement, the feeling was intensified. My palms were sweating as I rested my fingers on the ivory keys.

"Come in!"

The door popped open and Jody's head

appeared.

"Hi." She smiled.

"Hey, Jo. Come on in."

I knew I shouldn't have been beckoning her into my apartment. I'd just had the call I'd been waiting for, the chance at a shot in NYC, but my impulse had a bloody mind of its own.

She was too beautiful not to welcome in. Her curious gaze shot around the room as she padded across the floor in her pink socks. Yoga pants were never supposed to look that good on a woman. I shifted in my seat, thankful the piano was there to hide my lap from view.

Jody rested her forearms on the closed piano lid, placing the baby monitor beside her and smiling down at me.

I wanted to tell her. I wanted to let her know about the call, but I knew the second I opened my mouth, she'd scurry out of the room, scared off by the idea of holding me back.

Maybe she didn't have to.

Maybe she could actually be part of it.

The idea blossomed inside me, rising like helium until it filtered through every part of my brain with a jubilant shout.

"So, um." Jody tucked a curl behind her ear. "I wanted to come over and thank you for what you did this afternoon."

I shrugged, brushing my finger over middle C. "I heard her crying and I just wanted to help you out."

"You did. I've had a really shitty week and she

was tired and I thought my brain was going to implode."

I chuckled with her.

"You just cut all the tension like that." She clicked her fingers. "You made everything better."

"Nah-uh." I shook my head. "Olly did."

Her smile was sunshine. "Well, next time you see him, can you thank him for me?"

"It was just the right song for that moment," I murmured.

My heart was still nestled in my stomach; its pounding sent vibrations though my limbs. Jody could be my songbird. She was my muse. Why not get her to sing for me, as well? We could make this work, couldn't we?

"Have you always been like that? With a song for everything?"

"Yeah, yeah, I think I have." I nodded, scratching the stubble on my chin. "I remember, actually, as a kid I'd be walking along with my mum, and I'd see someone and they'd make me think of a song. She'd laugh at me and say, 'You don't just have a song for every moment, you've got a song for every*one*, as well.' And she was right, I can't meet people now without a song coming to mind."

"Oh, yeah?" Jody's head tipped, her long hair splashing over her shoulder as her eyes danced with mischief. "What song do you think about when you're dealing with Ms. Thornby?"

I grinned, pounding the keys and singing the first line of "Yakety Yak" by the Coasters.

A burst of musical laughter came out of her. "That's perfect! What about the Cray-Cray?"

"That's easy." My fingers sank into the keys and I belted out, "You drive me cra-zy!"

Jody's giggling increased, her shoulders shaking. "I'm sure your interpretation of that song is a little different to what Britney had in mind," she teased.

I laughed with her. "Yeah, well it's just that one line, repeated over and over in my head, so my version has a very different connotation than hers."

"I'm totally going to sing that now, every time I have to deal with him."

We grinned at each other, the electricity flowing between our locked gazes sparked with intensity. Jody broke first, looking down at the piano top and bobbing her shoulders.

"This is fun, tell me another one." She leaned forward, her perfect breasts squishing against her forearms; the milky white curve showing over the edge of her tank top made my mouth water.

"Um." I forced my eyes back to her face, although that didn't feel much safer. I cleared the tickle from my throat and clicked my fingers. "Oh, your sister, she always makes me hum "Titanium" by David Guetta for some reason."

Jody's lips rose with an awestruck smile. There was a look in her eyes I didn't quite understand, but I couldn't help thinking that I'd totally nailed that one.

"What about Angel?" she whispered.

My fingers hit the keys straight away, and I

played the opening baseline of "My Girl" by the Temptations, clicking my fingers and then singing, "I've got sunshine..." She quickly joined me and we sang through to the end of the first chorus.

Her voice was like honey, its sweet nectar intoxicating my senses.

"My dad used to sing that to me when I was little." Jody's smile was sad for a moment, but she shook the emotion off and grinned. "That's perfect for Angel."

"Yeah, it is."

She nipped the edge of her lip with her teeth, her cheeks flushing pink as she glanced back down at the piano top. "What about me?"

She was nervous asking.

Heck, I felt nervous responding. Should I tell her?

I scratched the back of my neck, feeling gun-shy and a little awkward when I tried to smile at her.

"You don't have a song for me?" Her nose wrinkled, her smile growing tight.

Oh, what the hell, she'd told me.

"Of course I do." I winked, my fingers hovering over the keys for just a second before I launched into Michael Buble's "Everything."

I sang to the end of the first chorus. I couldn't meet her gaze, but her eyes were on me the whole time. I could feel it. My voice petered out, my fingers coming to rest on the keys. My heart was back in my ribcage, thumping like a strobe light. Bloody hell, she needed to say something!

I drew in a quick breath and glanced her way,

ready to face whatever expression she might be wearing.

My chest restricted, my Adam's apple feeling huge in my throat when I tried to swallow.

Jody's eyes were glassy, a soft smile curving the edge of her lips. Pushing off the piano, she stepped over to me. I swiveled to face her, perching on the edge of the stool. She came to stand between my legs. I could sense her hesitancy, but that didn't stop her teeth from brushing over her lower lip and her fingers from gliding through my shaggy hair.

There weren't any words left. I sang her my heart...all I could do now was kiss her.

Stretching up, I lightly placed my fingers on her neck, running my thumb over her chin before pulling her toward me.

Our lips brushed, sparks flashing between our soft skin. She sighed against my mouth, her hands trailing down my head and coming to rest on my shoulders. I cupped her face, delicately holding her against me, and applied more pressure, my hungry tongue wanting to dive in without caution.

It took every ounce of restraint to hold back, let her make the next move. Her kiss seemed tentative for some reason, and I couldn't quite figure out why.

I held my ground, enjoying the sheer pressure of our mouths pressing together and forcing myself not to dream of more. Jody's taut muscles began to relax against me, her hesitation shifting. I felt the edge of her tongue skim my bottom lip.

My blood ignited, my limbs surging back into

vibration mode...and then the baby monitor squawked.

We jerked away from each other, the unexpected sound jolting us both.

I pressed my lips together, giving her an understanding smile.

Her lips parted as if to say something, but no words came out. Instead, she grabbed the monitor and headed back out the door, her fingers running lines over her lips as she went.

I stayed in my seat, unable to move until the door clicked shut behind her.

The first thing to twitch were my lips; they curved into a slow smile as my body dropped down to a simmer that felt warm and lush. Spinning back on the stool, my fingers quickly found the keys, and I picked up Jody's song where I'd left off, because she was all those things, and if I got to be her man, I'd sing this to her every day if she wanted me to.

TWENTY-FIVE

LEO

"You little ripper! Woohoo!" I jumped into Bobby's arms, giving him a hard slap on the back.

His mate liked the proposal! It was happy-dance time.

Bobby chuckled, slapping me back and pulling away from me. "I'm proud of you, kid, but don't get ahead of yourself. He still has to hear the music, and then has to like that, and then he'll want to hear more and pitch those to his buddies. This is going to be a long, slow process. You're gonna have to be patient."

"Yeah, yeah, I know, I know. But hearing back

after only three weeks is impressive right?"

"Yes, that is a good response time."

I giggled, a gleeful silly one that made me feel like a child, but I didn't care. This was perfect. Things were finally coming together.

"So, our job now is to make sure those songs come out as sellable as we can make them. You'll need to finish recording your best piece from the first act and see if you can't find yourself a few decent singers to make the demos."

"I've already got a lead in mind. She's a mezzo-soprano, perfect for the part."

I hadn't told Jody yet, but I would tonight. I no longer had any reason for hesitating. Since our first kiss we'd shared a dozen more. They were all short and fleeting, but that didn't make them any less addictive. I wanted more, I wasn't going to lie, but that was Jody's call, not mine. She'd already had one guy knock her up and leave her in the dust. I wasn't going to be like that. The little general may have a mind of his own, but I was stronger, and I'd rather die than hurt her.

She'd let me know when she was ready, I was sure of it. What I really wanted to do was shift to the idea that this casual kissing thing we had going on could easily become something more...maybe even something permanent. It scared the crap out of me to think that way, but I couldn't get the thought out of my mind...one that involved Broadway *and* my two girls.

Could we make it work?

I drove home pondering, my mind still

overflowing with questions as I took the lift to the top floor. Pausing in the corridor, I glanced at my door and then headed straight for Jody's.

"It's open," she called after my quick knock.

I frowned, walking through and shutting it behind me. "You know it's nearly ten, you should be locking your door after dark."

"I know." She shrugged. "But I thought there might be a chance that some hot guy would come knocking at my door, and I'm on the floor here folding laundry and I didn't want to have to get up." Her eyes twinkled.

I shook my head, grinning at her as I shrugged out of my jacket and threw it over the back of the couch.

Oh, man, she was wearing her foxy PJ pants again. Damn if they didn't undo me.

Dropping down beside her, I reached for a pair of baby socks and folded them together, hoping the menial task would cool the fiery heat pulsing through my veins.

"How was your day?" I asked.

"Oh, you know, the usual. Mr. Cray-Cray was yelling at pigeons again, Ms. Thornby found a speck of dust underneath her couch and nearly passed out, and Angel ate an ant. So, not a completely awful day."

I chuckled and reached for a yellow dress with a pink happy face flower on it.

"I did manage to start organizing Angel's birthday party for next weekend, so..." Her eyes danced over to mine, looking damn adorable.

"So?" I grinned at her.

She rolled her eyes, her head bobbling on her shoulders. "Do you want to come?"

I leaned forward and pecked her lips. "I'd love to."

Her smile was sunshine.

"How was your day?" She scrunched a hot pink G-string in her hand and threw it onto her pile.

Damn. I swallowed, flicking my eyes back to her and reminding myself why I'd popped in.

"Good." I nodded, trying to curb my excitement. "I heard from a guy in New York."

Jody gasped, dropping the shirt in her hands and spinning to face me. "And?"

A slow smile crept over my lips. "Well, the proposal I sent him sounds like it could be a goer."

She slapped my arm. "You've already sent a proposal to New York and you didn't tell me?"

"I was waiting to know more."

"You tell me next time." She pointed at me, her eyes narrowing.

I grabbed her finger and lightly tugged it, kissing the tip before letting her go. She grinned. "So, did they like it?"

"They're interested."

She squealed, jumping to her knees and wrapping her arms around me. "Oh my gosh, I'm so proud of you!"

I squeezed her waist, relishing the warm glow radiating through me. I loved hearing her say that.

She bounced back, her face still alight. "What's the next step?"

"Well, I have to record my best song from the first act with full orchestral arrangement, plus finish writing the last two songs. He has to like what I've sent and then pitch that to the money people and then we go from there."

Her smile faltered for a second, but she pulled it together, flashing me another broad grin.

"It's going to take a really long time, Jo." I rubbed her arm. "I'm not going anywhere in a hurry."

Her smile relaxed but not completely. We both knew what I wasn't saying, both trying to decide if we should go for whatever we had going on here, knowing that it most likely had an expiry date.

I frowned. Damn it, why should it have to have one!

"Sing for me." The words popped out fast and clear.

"What do you mean?" Jody's eyes danced.

"Be my demo singer. You're perfect for the main part."

"Really? You think so?"

"I know so." I chuckled, reaching for her face and rubbing my thumb over her cheekbone. "Some of these songs would suit your voice perfectly, and the one I want to send in first has your name written all over it." I didn't quite have it in me to tell her she'd been my muse, that everything had started from her. What if she hated the music?

No, that little truth nugget could be handed out later.

Jody sat back on her knees, sheer excitement

skittering over her expression. "You want me to sing your stuff for a demo?"

"I do." I smiled. "Do you want to?"

She gasped, covering her mouth and nodding. Reaching for me, she held my face in her hands and planted her lips on mine. The kiss was filled with zest and passion, more than she'd ever given me before. Her tongue dove into my mouth, her excited buzz flowing from her straight into me. I responded immediately, catching her tongue against mine. My core temperature skyrocketed. She tasted good. The heat inside her mouth was like an open flame. I was about to grab for her waist and pull her onto my lap when she jerked away from me.

"Sorry." She touched her lips with a shy smile. "I just got carried—"

I didn't let her finish. I dragged her back against me before she could say more, my hungry tongue devouring the taste I'd been craving. Jody sighed against my mouth, her arms wrapping around my shoulders as she scrambled onto my lap. My hands went roaming before I could stop them, sliding over the curve of her waist and coming to rest against her breasts. My thumbs brushed her nipples, her sugary sigh encouraging me to do it again. Her hands sped down my back, clawing under my shirt and sliding it up my torso, her light touch sending the little general into overdrive.

Our hot breaths mingled together, my fingers itching for a taste of her smooth skin. My thumb skimmed beneath her top, traveling up her body until I hit a cotton bra. Her nipples were hard beneath my touch, and I wanted to feel them with more than just my hands.

Tugging at the material, I yanked her shirt north. Jody raised her arms for me, letting me lift it over her head. I smiled at the bright purple bra cupping her breasts. It was covered in starbursts and way too pretty to just rip off.

She giggled, tipping backward and lying against the mound of unfolded laundry. I ran my hands up her smooth waist, relishing the contours of her body. She felt fantastic.

Her hands came around my neck, and she pulled me on top of her, her legs wrapping around my hips. I didn't know what I'd let loose with my invitation to let her sing, but I liked it.

Our tongues wove together, the heated sensation scorching my senses. Her legs shifted, her heels digging into my butt, and her moan grew as I pressed my jeans between her legs, the desire in both of us escalating quickly. I felt near blinded by passion. If I didn't pull it together quickly, I wouldn't be able to control myself.

I broke our kiss, resting my forehead against hers. "You taste too good."

"So do you." She licked her bottom lip, her panting sending shockwaves of desire pulsing through me. I ground my hips, pressing the rock-hard general against the tender spot between her thighs. Damn that felt good. Jody closed her eyes, her head tipping back as her fingers clasped the back of my neck and a sweet moan eased out of her mouth. I wanted to do it again and again. I wanted to hear the sound of our flesh slapping together and feel that scorching ecstasy of her silky insides encasing me...but I couldn't.

It took all my willpower to detach her legs from around me and sit back. The little general was throwing a tantrum as I kept him locked up behind my zipper. I squirmed on the floor, forcing myself to utter the words I didn't want to say. "We can't, Jo, I'm sorry."

Her face blanched, her eyes rounding with embarrassment as she sat up and scrambled away from me, knocking over the neat piles of washing with her butt. Her fingers were shaking as she ran a hand through her hair and reached for her T-shirt.

"Yeah, you're probably right. It's a bad idea." She pulled on her shirt and looked so dejected, I kicked myself for not explaining quicker.

"Jo." I reached for her again, lightly holding the back of her neck. "It's not that I don't want to. I really, *really* do, but I just had to stop before I couldn't."

Her eyes dipped to the floor and she nodded.

"I don't—" I sighed. "I don't have any protection." I was embarrassed to admit it. What guy with a neighbor as hot as Jody (who I'd already kissed!) wouldn't have protection! I winced. "I haven't been with a woman since Gerry, and every time we kiss you keep pulling away, and I just figured there was no hurry, because you didn't want to."

"I want to." She clutched my forearm, looking

up at me with those big beautiful eyes. "Oh, man, I want you so bad, but I just feel like I don't...deserve you." I was forced to let her go as she shuffled away from me. "I don't want to hold you back. You're a good guy who would give up his dreams because you wouldn't want to let anyone down. I don't want to be the thing that stops you from getting everything you want."

I closed my eyes, remembering her drunken confession. "Jo," I sighed. "You—" I clicked my tongue, shaking my head with a grin. "Now who's being thick as bloody pig shit?" I threw her an exasperated look.

"Excuse me!" Her mock horror was a picture.

I laughed at her, refusing to take it back. As if she didn't deserve me. Crikey, she had no idea! My laughter was cut short by a pair of socks in the face. I flinched, but recovered quickly from the attack, snaffling a pair of her panties off the pile and biffing them at her. They landed straight in her laughing mouth. Her shock of surprise got me chuckling again, and then it was all on. Grabbing up handfuls of ammo, we started an all-out laundry war, our raucous antics soon waking Angel.

We hissed, both whispering at each other to shut up while we tried to hamper our giggles. Angel's cries increased.

"Just go." Jody giggled, pointing at the door.

I nodded and crept from the room, my stomach still quivering with laughter and my body ignited by the idea that the foxy girl next door wanted every inch of me. Oh, man, I couldn't wait to share it with her.

TWENTY-SIX

JODY

I looked at the recipe again, my forehead crinkling as I tried to remember how many quarter cups of flour I'd already put into the mixing bowl. Dubiously glancing at the white mound of flour resting on top of the wet ingredients, I bit my lip and figured one more would probably be right. I really needed to buy more measuring cups, of different sizes, so I didn't have to count all the time.

I was annoyed with myself for losing track, but I couldn't help it. My mind had been a mess all week...a giddy, excited mess. I'd spent most of it hanging out with Leo, learning the melody and lyrics for "I Want The World."

"I want the world, I want it all, ready to jump even if I fall, 'cause I'm a dream chaser...which one will come true?" I held the note, letting my voice fade as the music swelled around me.

I looked over at Leo, my nose wrinkling. "Was that okay?"

"Bloody perfect, Jo. You're bringing this song to life!"

I grinned, leaning against the piano, my favorite spot in his apartment. Glancing over Leo's shoulder, I checked on Angel. She was playing on the big carpet square behind him, munching on a new set of blocks Morgan had bought her. Dribble painted half of them, while the rest were in a stack that was seconds away from toppling over.

My insides swelled as reality dawned on me suddenly.

I was in a perfect moment.

Angel was happy. Leo was playing. I was singing. It couldn't get better.

Picking up the music, I skimmed the words again while Leo played through the accompaniment.

"So, what's this musical about?"

He glanced up, a slow smile cresting over his lips. "Well..." He cleared his throat, adjusting his jeans and wriggling along the piano bench so I could sit down beside him.

I slid into place as Leo started softly playing and speaking at the same time. "It's about a girl who's dying. She's on her deathbed with a raging fever and she starts to have all these dreams. At first it's kind of scary, but then she realizes that she's dreaming about what her different futures could look like. She meets this old wise lady, kind of like a fairy godmother, who tells her she needs to find the dream worth living for and so she sets out on this journey."

I lifted the music in my hand. "That's this song, isn't it?"

"Yeah." He nodded, his fingers tinkling over the keys. "She accepts the lady's advice and becomes a dream chaser, and the musical takes her to all these different places, and she gets a taste of the life she could have, depending on which dream she chooses to pursue."

"And which dream does she choose?" I nudged him with my shoulder.

He stopped playing, turning to me with a twinkle in his eye. "The music, of course. A stage, a spotlight, a chorus of back-up singers."

"Ahh, so your dream then."

He chuckled. "I don't want the stage, Jo." His hand rested lightly on my face, his lips moving toward mine and teasing me by stopping a quarter-inch from contact. "I want to see you on a stage, singing my songs," he whispered, his lips pressing against mine.

My insides buzzed as I relived the moment It'd only gotten better from there. We'd spent the next day at a recording studio downtown where I'd blissfully acquainted myself with a microphone. Yes, I'd gotten to spend all day in a recording studio singing. It had been the best day ever. The song was beautiful, powerful, and so much fun to sing. It was the perfect key for me, making my voice sound vivid and alive.

I'd been in heaven.

Angel had come with us, playing on the floor and being carried around by different assistants and sound guys. She'd had a blast and won everyone over with her cute little smile. Although by the time we'd gotten home, she was so grouchy it took me two hours to get her to sleep. I had to concede that a full day in a recording studio was probably not the best thing for my baby.

Leo had sent the song off yesterday, and we were both trying to distract ourselves with other things and not obsess over what the guy in New York might say. Leo was practically glued to his piano stool every second he could spare, working on arrangements. He was hoping to record two more pieces in case the guy wanted more. He wanted to be as prepared as possible.

I was secretly hoping he'd ask me to record more for him, although I'd have to think of something to do with Angel.

Morgan had taken her for me today. Popped over in the morning and said she wanted to spend a little quality time with her niece while Mommy got the place ready for her birthday party the next day. I'd decided to go for a very low-key affair, just inviting family and Leo. Angel would be the only kid, but I was still going to make her a pink and purple butterfly cake.

"Right," I muttered, pausing to point the remote at my stereo and fast-forward the song. Shuffle play was such a farce. I knew I hadn't listened to every song in my playlist, yet it continued to repeat ones I'd been listening to all morning. I tried not to let it bug me as I read the next step of the recipe.

Dumping in the rest of the ingredients, I picked up the spatula and gave the batter a stir. I frowned, hoping it was actually supposed to be as runny as it was. I'd never baked a cake before. Cookies were my specialty, and even they weren't that great. I winced, hoping I wasn't going to poison anyone at the party by accident.

I ran my finger over the next instruction and turned to snatch the baking tins out of the dish rack. Following each step to the letter, I prepared the tins and once the batter was in, I placed them in the oven. I checked the temperature and set the timer for forty-five minutes.

I was just turning back to clean up the countertop when the front door clicked open.

"Hey." Leo's head came into view and my insides sizzled the way they always did.

"Hey." I grinned, licking the spatula and smearing chocolate batter on my face. I blushed, rushing to wipe it off.

Leo chuckled, closing the door with his butt and walking across to me. "Where's Angel?"

"With Aunt Morgan. They've gone out for a girly lunch."

"Nice." Leo nodded, his eyes sparkling as he drank me in. I was wearing an old cotton sundress and bare feet. His gaze made me feel like I was dressed for the prom.

"So, what are you doing here?"

He shrugged. "I just thought I'd come over and see if you needed a hand with birthday prep."

"I've just put Angel's cake in the oven, which has been my main nightmare. Now I'm gonna clean up and start praying it doesn't taste like doggy do-do."

He laughed at my joke, crossing the room toward me.

I picked up the bowl and popped it in the sink, stealing one last lick of chocolate batter before spinning back to clear off the island.

Leo's laughter grew louder when I turned.

"What?" I smiled at his expression.

He came around the island. I swiveled to watch him lazily walk toward me, his adorable half-smile not shifting until he'd boxed me in. My palms pressed against the edge of the counter, my nerves leap-frogging over each other. He'd become so damn sexy these past couple of months, I could barely think straight around him. His strong arms rested on either side of me, his white teeth flashing as he leaned forward and sucked my chin.

Leaning back, he licked his lips. "Definitely not doggy do-do."

I giggled, wiping my chin and trying to regulate my heartbeat. Leo standing this close always did things to me. His warm breath tickled my nose as his lips hovered above mine. He was going to kiss me again, and this time, I wasn't going to pull back.

My skin prickled, goosebumps rippling over my belly. Heat pooled between my legs at the thought of what he'd felt like the night of the laundry fight. I'd been fantasizing about it ever since, but we hadn't had a chance to do anything. Between rehearsals, Angel, and running a building...but was it now? Was this our chance?

My breath quickened as I gazed up at him. Our smiles grew in unison and our mouths reached for each other. His lips were soft in contrast to his short stubble. The whiskers tickled my tongue before I dove into the hot oasis of his mouth. Our tongues swirled around each other, a hot-heady concoction. He moaned and tipped his head, deepening the kiss. His hands went straight for my hair, digging into my thick locks before shimmying down my body, gliding over my hips until they reached the bare thigh below my dress. His fingertips danced across my skin, teasing me as he slowly worked his way up to my butt.

I grinned against his lips, tugging at his shirt and forcing him to stop and lift his arms. I threw the fabric behind me, knocking the broken eggshells onto the floor.

"Whoops." I snickered, turning away from the mess and running my hands over his naked torso.

I shook my head, biting my lip in awe of his rippled torso. I loved the ridges of his muscles, the way they dipped and curved beneath my fingers. They were hard and beautifully shaped, his nipples erect as I skimmed my thumbs over them. With a cheeky grin, I leaned forward and licked each one, sucking lightly before trailing kisses over his chest. His groans of pleasure fueled my tongue as I painted his body, working my way up to his neck.

Leo gripped my hips and lifted me onto the counter. With quick hands, he pulled my dress north. I raised my arms, making his job easier. His eyes roamed my body as he flicked the light fabric to the side, knocking the open flour packet over. White dust billowed in the air, coating the counter, the floor, and the edge of my right leg.

"Oops." Leo didn't even look sorry as he ran his fingers through the white dust on my skin, painting a pattern with his finger, then brushing the dust off on my quivering belly.

I reciprocated his cocky grin, brushing my teeth over my lower lip and pulling him toward me. Our bodies slapped together, his hard stomach kissing the insides of my thighs. The heat in my core ignited as our tongues collided once more. Leo's wide hands skimmed up my back, unhooking my bra and pulling it off. He threw it over his shoulder, and I heard it plop into the mixing bowl.

He cupped my breasts, rolling my hard nipples between his fingers and making me shudder. A delighted whimper skipped off my tongue and straight into his mouth. He chuckled, his hot tongue sliding over my lips before moving down my neck and exploring my body. My fingers wove through his hair as he teased my nipples, waves of pleasure firing down to my toes. I moaned, a loud, shameless cry that filled the kitchen. There was no sleeping baby to worry about waking. We weren't locked away in a singing studio trying to be quiet so no one could hear us. Nothing had to be hidden about this encounter and it was liberating.

Leo's lips turned my insides to putty, his fingers creeping around the edges of my panties and tugging lightly at them. I raised my butt, letting him slide them off me. He kissed my knee as I slid it out of the fabric. Running his hands up my leg, his thumb gently pressed the soft flesh of my inner thigh. My underwear went flying behind him, landing on the handle of the pantry door. I giggled, finding the strewn clothing hilarious, but the sound was cut short by Leo's fingers. They caught me by surprise, sliding inside of me. I leaned my head back, gasping at the sweet intrusion. I hadn't been touched in a really long time, and I'd never been touched this gently before. With Stefan it had been always a quick rush, his fingers digging into me as a speedy precursor to get to what he really wanted. Leo, on the other hand, was taking his sweet time about this and I can tell ya, it was an easy win for the Aussie bloke. Holy sweet spot!

His thumb caressed me softly— a teasing tickle that had me seeing stars. Heady vibrations thrummed through my body as my breathing grew to rapid pants of pleasure. My fingers scrambled for his belt buckle, an urgent desire overtaking me. I wanted to feel him, run my fingers over his tight, smooth skin. Leo pulled back, letting me rid him of his jeans.

I gazed down at his naked form, my lips parting.

Holy...there was no word. He was just...wow.

It occurred to me that this was the first time I'd

ever had sex fully naked. Stefan was always paranoid about being caught, so our clothing was only ever pulled apart, making the essentials accessible. But this...this was—I stopped, soaking in Leo's body, drinking in the uninhibited beauty of this moment.

With a wicked smile, I wrapped my fingers around his length, enjoying the groan rumbling in his throat as I stroked him. He closed his eyes, his fingers picking up speed and driving into me, his thumb working fast circles that had me gasping for air. Stars continued to burst in front of my vision until my body became a limbless wreck. I couldn't breathe as an orgasm rocketed through me. My hands slapped against the countertop and I threw my head back, letting out a feral cry.

My limbs shook as I found the outer edge of the counter and clung to it. Leo kept going—sucking, kissing, stroking until I couldn't take it anymore. My knees came up, digging into his ribcage, my words coated with a pleading tone. "I don't suppose you have...?"

"You better believe it." He let me go, a bittersweet reprieve, and scrambled for his jeans, yanking a condom out of the back pocket. "I bought them the day after our laundry fight." He grinned, ripping it open with his teeth. "I've been carrying them on me ever since."

I giggled, sitting up and taking it off him. "Always be prepared, right?" I slid it on.

"And optimistic." His breathy chuckle in my ear charged the nerves already zinging through my body.

"I really like that about you," I whispered against his mouth, our kiss cutting off the final word.

His fingers grazed down my spine, tickling my skin with a soft caress that grew firm. His hands cupped my butt, lifting me against him. His length pressed against my inner thigh, and then slid inside me, a smooth motion that sucked the breath out of my lungs.

His arms wrapped tightly around me, my eyes closing as I tried to wrap my brain around the fact I was making love to Leo Sinclair. My fingers scraped across his back, my teeth skimming the flesh of his shoulder. He felt divine, better than anything I'd ever had.

There was a soft devotedness to this moment, and it made me realize that as high as Stefan could get me, this was a whole new plane. Although Leo hadn't said it, I could feel his sole focus in this encounter was to give me pleasure.

It always felt the other way around with Stefan. He'd rush through the foreplay in order to get me on my back, but Leo was taking his sweet time about it. Even now, inside me, I could feel his restraint, wanting it to last as long as possible.

Leo's breathing grew heavy in my ear, his hands on my back shifting to my butt. I raised my knees, leaning back against the countertop. The move shifted angles, heightening the already overpowering sensations coursing through me. My hands shot across the bench, the measuring cup and spoon firing off the smooth surface and dropping to the kitchen floor with a clatter.

Neither of us laughed this time. Our eyes were locked together, saying a thousand things as he gripped my hips and filled me, our bodies moving in a rhythmic dance that only we knew the moves to. His fingers dug into my flesh as the tempo increased, the muscles in his neck straining tight. I arched my back, the pressure inside me swelling like a bubbling volcano. We cried out together, the burst of fire and energy that tore through our bodies, leaving us spent and satisfied.

TWENTY-SEVEN

LEO

Jody lay on the floor, naked and glorious beside me. Her skin was coated in flour, our second romp on the floor getting messy. I hadn't intended to jump her again quite so quickly, but when she'd gotten the cakes out of the oven wearing nothing but a mitt, I caught one look at her perfect behind, and I had to have her again. As soon as she'd laid those cakes down, I'd pulled her against me and we'd dropped to the floor.

I perched up on my elbow, gazing down at her, my hand resting lightly on her hip. Geez, she was beautiful.

Cody Simpson was singing "Love," and it was impossible not to feel the emotion as I looked at her.

I couldn't quite form the words, my throat too clogged with emotion. When I'd left Gerry, I had accepted the idea that I may never fall in love again. I wasn't the type of guy who liked to sleep around. I'd been raised to believe that sex was meant to be saved for a committed relationship and I'd stuck with it.

I guessed that meant Jody and I were in a committed relationship, and as much as I thought that idea might scare me, it didn't. In fact, I kind of loved it.

Her smile was sweet as she reached for my face, running her fingers through my stubble.

"I love you," she whispered.

My smile grew to blinding. I was surprised she could still look at me without squinting. I squeezed her hip. "I know, you've already told me."

"What?" Her expression bunched with confusion.

I chuckled, almost wishing I hadn't said anything. I winced before clearing my throat and getting it over with. "That night you came home drunk after Sean's birthday party. When I was trying to get your trashed-self into bed, you confessed all."

Her lips parted, her eyes bulging wide.

I countered her expression with a soft kiss, rubbing my nose against hers. "Hearing you say it out loud, even though you didn't even realize you were telling me..." I shook my head with a wry chuckle. "It just made me realize that I felt the same way."

"But that was weeks ago. Why didn't you do anything about it?"

"I did. I sang you a song and kissed you."

She rolled her eyes. "I meant, why didn't you say anything?"

I brushed the back of my knuckles over her cheek. "I wanted the moves to come from you. I didn't want to be the guy who pressured you. I'd never hurt you, Jo. I never, ever want you to feel forced into anything you don't want to do."

Her mushy look made my heart squeeze, her bright blue eyes growing glassy as she wrapped her fingers around my neck and pulled me in for a kiss. It was slow and lingering, until her foot skimmed up the back of my leg.

I leaned away from her and she giggled, her eyebrow arching. "How many of those condoms do you have left in your pocket?"

We didn't have time to find out. Before I could even form my answer, the front door started jiggling. Our bodies tensed in unison, freezing with a split-second of fright before we scrambled into action. Jody plucked my clothes off the floor, throwing them at me and shoving me toward the pantry. Flinging the door back, she pushed me inside, slamming the door closed before I could protest. I had no room to move in the tight black space, so I had to hold my clothes against my chest and hope like hell Jody had managed to throw her dress on in time.

"Man, that door is a pest!" Morgan's voice filled the room, followed by the definitive whack of a door closing. "You really need to get it fixed, Jo-Jo."

"Ah, yeah. I know, it's on my list."

"Are you okay? You look...flustered."

"Nope." Jody accentuated the P, giving herself away.

Come on, girly, you can do better than that, I thought to myself.

"I mean, baking can get me all up the fluster a little."

Morgan's voice was narrow and cautious as it drew closer to the kitchen. "I can see that. You're covered in flour."

I pressed my lips together, grinding my teeth to stop myself from chuckling. The kitchen looked like a hurricane had blown through it. If only Morgan knew the truth.

My body quaked with mirth. I clutched the clothes, digging my fingers into the material and forcing myself not to lose it.

"So, how's my Angel?"

I smiled at the sweet tone Jody's voice took on when she greeted her daughter. Angel squealed and started babbling.

"She needs a change," Morgan said.

"Okay, cool. I might just go ahead and put her straight into the bath. Would you like a bath, cupcake?" Angel giggled and I could picture Jody lifting her in the air. The continued giggles made me think Jody was throwing her up and down, rubbing their noses together. I recognized the sounds.

"Do you want me to stay and help you clean up?" Morgan sounded reluctant, but from what Jody had said, she wasn't the kind of person to let misgivings stop her from doing something.

"No, that's cool. You've got a dance class soon, don't you?"

"Yeah, but if I hurry..."

"No, don't worry about it. I'll, um, do it later."

"O-kay."

"Morgan," Jody chided. "The house will be clean for the party tomorrow. Don't worry about it. As if I'd let Dad walk in and see this."

"Yeah, sure, but call me if you want me over early, okay?"

"Will do," Jody sing-songed.

I held my breath, listening for sounds around the room. I heard the creak of what I assumed was the bathroom door and then the front door opened and shut. Letting out a sigh, I shouldered the pantry open, dropping my clothes to the floor and snagging out my jeans.

I didn't bother with undies, just slid the denim up my thighs and froze still as the front door jerked open again.

"Hey, Jody, I—"

Morgan jolted to a stop, her eyes rounding as she saw me. I quickly pulled my pants up and zipped the fly, clearing my throat and raising my hand in a wave.

"Hey, Morgan."

Her eyes narrowed, her left hand landing on her hip. I felt like I'd just been caught stealing cookies by the food police.

I forced a smile, scratching the back of my head.

Morgan's jaw worked to the side, her eyebrow arching as she soaked in the mess of the kitchen. Her eyes bulged, and I followed her gaze, spotting Jody's bra half-dangling out of the mixing bowl. If she hadn't worked it out by now she was a bloody idiot, and one thing I knew for certain was that Morgan was sharp as a tack.

She pointed at the cooling cake tins. "Am I gonna want to eat that birthday cake tomorrow?"

I glanced at it. "Oh, um, yeah, no, cake's good. We...it's...we were—" My fingers waved over the bench and then the floor, my words evaporating under her stern gaze. "It'll be good."

I dug my hands into my pockets and rocked back on my heels.

Her teeth caught the edge of her lip as she tried to fight a smile, her sharp nose wrinkling.

My chest loosened.

"You know, much to my surprise, I'm actually okay with this." Her head tipped to the side, her soft expression going hard as she glared at me. "But you break my kid sister's heart, I break your balls."

My head shot back in surprise, before bobbing. "I believe you."

"You should. My fiancé could kick your ass."

"Got it." I winked with what I thought was my most charming grin.

Her smile dropped, her expression going steely as she crossed her arms.

I cleared my throat again, vanquishing the charm and going for the most sincere look I could muster. It wasn't hard; I meant exactly what I was about to say. "I have no intention of breaking Jo's heart, I promise."

Satisfied, Morgan nodded and disappeared back out the door. I let out a sigh, sagging against the pantry for a minute. That chick was seriously titanium. Lucky for me, I was one sucker for Jody Pritchett, and after the session we'd just spent together in the kitchen, I was pretty sure I'd be staying that way for a good long while...hopefully forever.

TWENTY-EIGHT

JODY

I couldn't stop smiling. How could I?

I was giddy, gleeful...like a giggling school kid with a major crush. Except this time it wasn't just a crush, it was full-blown love. A *mutual* love.

Leo stayed and cleaned up the entire kitchen for me while I settled Angel.

If that's not love, I don't know what is.

The door jiggled, and Angel and I turned at the sound, our smiles simultaneous as Leo stepped into the apartment. He grinned at us, his gaze heating with passion as our eyes connected. My belly quivered while my mind replayed the scene in the kitchen from the day before. I'd never be able to look at my kitchen counter the same way again.

Angel's squeal of delight broke the spell. She wriggled out of my arms. I stood her on her feet, watching her sway. Her arms went up in the air, and she took a few teetering steps forward, going for Leo. She nearly made it, plopping onto her bottom and smiling at our cheers.

"That was five steps, cupcake." I ruffled her fuzz. "Clever girl."

Her eight little teeth appeared as she clapped her hands and giggled. Leo picked her up, throwing her in the air and catching her again. She bobbed in his arms, squealing with excitement. It's like she knew this was her special day.

I'd managed to make her cake, sort of. Actually, I'd kind of mangled it a little. The two butterfly wings were different sizes, the second growing smaller and smaller as I tried to trim the cake to the right shape. I'd stayed up until past midnight trying to ice the damn thing. Poor Angel, she was never going to get fancy cakes out of me. Hers looked like it'd been decorated by a five-year-old.

Leo came around beside me and peered down at the pink and purple creation. He nodded, his lips pressing together, highlighting his small dimple.

"Shut up," I mumbled.

He wrapped his arm around me and kissed the side of my head. "At least we know it doesn't taste like doggy do-do."

I snorted, my tummy quaking with giggles. Leo's smile grew as he turned me to face him, leaning down to kiss my lips while Angel explored our ears with her little fingers. We chuckled against each other, only being ripped apart by the uncomfortable throat clearing from the doorway.

"Oh, hey, you guys." I forced a bright smile, ignoring the frown on Dad's face.

This was his first time here and yeah, he didn't know about Leo.

I wiped my lips with a shaky finger and came around the counter to hug Grandma Deb. Dad didn't even look my way as he brushed past me and took Angel out of Leo's grasp.

I shot a glare at the back of my father's head. Grandma Deb gave my shoulder a squeeze. I took courage from her reassuring smile and moved toward the kitchen.

"Dad, this is Leo...my neighbor and boss, and my...boyfriend." Dad's withering gaze had me whispering the last word.

I looked away, tucking a curl behind my ear and wishing for a moment that the floor would open up and chow me down for lunch.

Leo coughed. I glanced up in time to see him extend his hand. "Nice to meet you, Marshall."

"It's Mr. Pritchett." He ended his three-second greeting with a grunt that made me want to punch him. Crossing my arms, I stared him down with a pointed glare that he couldn't miss. He turned away from it, distracting himself with Angel.

Grandma Deb jumped in with her usual charm, wrapping her arms around Leo and kissing his cheek.

"So nice to meet you, Leo. I hear you're a song writer." I loved her for it, but it didn't take away the sting of Dad's reaction. My eyes shot back to him on the floor with my daughter. They were stacking blocks together, Angel showing off her clapping skills while Dad cheered her on.

I loved that he was so good with her. She hadn't seen him in weeks, and within five minutes of his attention, she was gazing at him with that adoring look in her eye. He grinned down at her, tipping her nose and making her laugh.

I stood juxtaposed between outright fury and a desire to clasp my hands together and say, "Awwww."

It wasn't fair. Why did she get all his sugar and I was left feeling like the bad guy? Marching into the kitchen, I busied myself with straightening the plates and unwrapping food.

"What can I help you with?" Leo whispered in my ear.

I couldn't talk. I was too mad at my dad for dismissing the best thing that had ever happened to me. I saw that look in his eyes.

First your teacher, now your boss? That was what his dark gaze had shouted at me. I just knew it.

Leo's hand came to rest on my lower back, his soft lips pressing into my hair. "Take a breath, foxy. It's going to be okay."

"I just hate that he was so rude to you." My whisper was harsh and tight.

"He doesn't know me yet. I'll win him over."

I glanced behind me, catching Leo's little wink.

My heart started tap-dancing when he leaned down and brushed his lips against the crook of my neck. I wanted to turn in his arms and lavish him with a kiss but was distracted by the arrival of Morgan and Sean.

I hugged them both and introduced the guys to each other.

My future brother-in-law gave Leo an amused smile as they shook hands. I threw my sister a questioning frown, until my eyes bulged large.

"You told him!" I mouthed.

She rolled her eyes. "Of course I did. I tell my fiancé everything."

Her cheeks tinged pink as she said the word fiancé, which was actually kind of adorable, but I was still mad at her. I'd nearly died when Leo told me Morgan had come back in and seen him naked then told him she'd break his balls. Honestly!

"He won't say anything," Morgan assured me, squeezing my upper arm. I flicked her hand off me and went to answer the door, relieved that Cole and Ella had arrived. Her sweet, oblivious smile told me Morgan had kept her lips zipped with my best friend, but I knew it wouldn't last for long. I'd have to get in and tell Ella before my big sister did.

Thankfully, the day was not about my sex-capade with Leo, and all about my precious Angel who was one. One whole year. My family lavished her with presents and love. We sang her "Happy Birthday" and she spat out her candle, with a little help from me. Ella and Sean snapped way too many photos, but it was the first time we'd actually had the chance to get some family shots.

"Here, Leo, do you mind taking a group shot?" Ella passed him her camera.

"Yeah, of course." He jumped up while we got ourselves positioned.

Angel was sitting on Grandpa's lap. I made sure I stayed on the other side, putting Morgan between me and my father. The only time he'd smiled throughout the afternoon was when he was interacting with Angel. As soon as she was out of range, he spent his time firing rocket glares at Leo and flicking a few my way, as well.

What the hell was his problem anyway!

"Say cheese!"

We all did as we were told, laughing at Leo while he clicked his fingers and tried to get Angel to look at the camera.

"Put it on timer and come in." I flicked my hand, shuffling closer to Morgan so Leo could perch on the edge of the seat.

"Why would he do that? He's not family." Dad's voice stopped Leo in his tracks and dropped an awkward bomb into the room that was impossible to recover from.

There was a heavy silent beat as Leo stopped fiddling with the camera timer. I willed myself not to lose it.

"He's family to me," I finally said, although my voice didn't carry the strength I wanted it to.

"Really? Because I've never met him before."

"Well, maybe if you'd come to visit, you would have."

"Maybe if you'd invited me, I would have come to visit!"

"Why would I invite you?" I shot out of my chair. "So you could come in here and tell me everything I'm doing wrong with my life? Tell me how I'm one big screw-up who threw everything away?"

Morgan's eyes bulged at me, telling me to shut it.

I ignored her, clicking my fingers in the air. "Oh, no, that's right, you don't say stuff like that to me, because you don't like talking to me anymore. I've let you down and broken your heart so badly that you can't even stand to have a conversation with me! Instead you say it all with your eyes, throwing evils at my boyfriend, frowning every time you see me. You know why I haven't invited you over yet? Because I didn't want to be made to feel like this! Marshall Pritchett's little fuck-up daughter."

I spun before the tears could burn me. Like hell I was letting them fall in front of my dad. I sped down to my room, slamming the door shut behind me and cursing myself for ruining Angel's birthday. I said *fuck* in front of her, too! What the hell was wrong with me!

"And the mother of the year award goes to..." I mumbled sarcastically, gripping the edge of my bed and wishing the day would just disappear.

My entire body was buzzing, my muscles quivering with tension. I'd obviously had that little outburst locked up for a while. I'd surprised myself by letting it all spew out in front of everyone. I just hadn't been able to contain it anymore.

I didn't want Leo to be another thing to add to Dad's list against me.

Leo was my saving grace, and I didn't want Dad screwing it up.

"You don't need Dad for that," I muttered, flinging myself back on the bed and covering my face with my arm.

The door creaked open. I tensed, too scared to see who it was.

"You okay?" Ella sat down beside me, her tiny hand rubbing my leg.

"No." I sniffed.

"Don't feel bad. You needed to get that stuff off your chest."

"Not in front of everybody," I whined. "I just humiliated myself."

Ella lay down beside me, resting her head against my shoulder and wrapping her arm around me. "You're not a fuck-up," she whispered.

A dry, breathy giggle spurted out of me. "I think that could be argued."

I could feel Ella's cheeks rising with a smile. "Don't underestimate yourself." She squeezed my waist. "And don't let your dad's issues ruin what you've got...a precious daughter and a gorgeous guy who obviously cares about you."

"I don't get my dad. What's his problem anyway? Ever since I dropped out of college, he hasn't looked at me the same."

Ella sighed, wrapping one of her big brown curls around her finger. "I don't know, I think he was just excited that you were getting to go off and live your dreams...and then it all came crashing down around you. I wonder if his anger is just a front for his fear."

"What's he got to be afraid of?" I spat.

"I don't think he's afraid for him, he's afraid for you. He busted his ass making sure you got every opportunity you could. He knew how much you wanted that stage, and he was going to do everything in his power to make it happen."

"But then I kept the baby."

"He loves Angel, though."

"I know, but..." I held my breath for a beat, not wanting to ask a question that had been flickering in the back of my mind since the day I'd seen that line turn blue on my pregnancy test. "Do you think he worries I'm going to turn into my mother?"

"You're not your mother," Ella whispered fiercely, but we both knew that wasn't the total truth. I was so like my mother it wasn't even funny. Same big blue eyes, same blonde hair, same singing voice, same hopes, same dreams! The list was endless...and terrifying.

I swallowed, my jaw working to the side as images of Dad's heartbreak filtered through me.

"You don't have to be like her," Ella murmured. "You're stronger than her, and you love Leo. I don't know if your mom ever really loved your dad. It's different for you, right?"

I nodded, running my fingers into my hair and trying to believe her. It was different. I did love Leo, like seriously loved him, and... "Leo loves me."

Ella jerked, popping up onto her elbow and flicking my arm out of the way. "He told you that?"

Her dancing smile made me grin.

I nodded. "Pretty much, after we made..."

Ella gasped, her lips parting with glee. "When? Where? Tell me everything!" she squealed.

My face scrunched. I could feel my cheeks burning as I admitted, "On the kitchen counter and then the floor. It was..." I sighed. "Ella, it was amazing, like nothing compared to...you know...and he was pretty good."

"Oh my gosh!" Ella threw her head back. "You little vixen, the kitchen counter!"

I slapped my hand over her loud exclamation.

"Sorry." Her giggling reply was muffled.

"Anyway, apparently the night I got totally wasted at Sean's party, I came home and blurted that I loved him, and he said he felt the same way."

"Awww." Ella pulled my hand off her mouth. "That is so sweet...and he's so good with Angel."

"I know." I smiled, my heart feeling like Play-Doh.

"I'm happy for you, Jo-Jo. You deserve it."

My smile grew tight and eventually faded with my sigh. "Why can't my dad say that?"

Ella shrugged, her expression full of sorrow. "Maybe one day he will."

I shook my head, gazing back up at the ceiling. I couldn't imagine it.

TWENTY-NINE

LEO

Marshall barely said two words to me while he was here, and the look he threw me as he was leaving was pretty black, too. I felt bad for him, actually. Jody had ripped him a new one, that's for sure. It was so out of character for her that it made me think there must have been a heck of a lot more going on under the surface, stuff I had yet to learn.

Jody never really spoke much about her father, and now I knew why.

I finished sweeping the floor and popped the broom down the edge of the fridge where Jody kept it. Wiping my hands on my backside, I turned to see her walk into the room. She'd exchanged her skinny jeans for her PJ bottoms and was looking adorable as per usual.

"Angel asleep?"

"Yeah." Jody nodded, rubbing her forehead and giving me a sad smile.

"Come 'ere, foxy." I pulled her against me, kissing her head and leaning my cheek against her hair.

"I'm sorry about today. I should have kept my damn mouth shut."

I rubbed her back. "Hey, you obviously needed to get it off your chest."

"But not in front of everybody!" Her voice was muffled against my shirt.

I squeezed her back and led her over to the couch. Plopping onto it, I pulled her into my lap and snuggled her against me.

"What happened with your dad?"

"We used to be so close, but then I..." Jody sucked in a ragged breath. "My mom left when I was ten. She moved to Vegas to pursue her dreams of becoming a singer, said she'd given everything she could and..." Her blonde curls tussled against my shoulder as she shook her head. I could feel the pain rippling off her. "She couldn't take it anymore. It kind of threw our house into turmoil. Morgan kept us all together with her practicality and strength."

I hummed the chorus from "Titanium," unable to help myself.

Jody grinned. "Nailed it."

I chuckled, tucking a curl behind her ear so I could see her face better.

"I think Dad always blamed himself. They got pregnant unexpectedly with Morgan, and when she was born he proposed and she's impulsive, like me. She said yes and locked herself into a life she never wanted." Jody's forehead crinkled. "I think when I got into theater in high school it was a redeeming chance for Dad. He'd denied his wife everything she wanted, and he wasn't going to let that happen to his little ray of sunshine." A tear slipped down her cheek and her lips wobbled. "That's what he always used to call me, and he hasn't said it once since I told him I was pregnant."

I used my thumb to wipe away her tears.

She sniffed and gave me a shaky smile. "I think he feels like I sold myself short by keeping Angel, and even though he loves her, he can't get past the fact that I've given up my dreams...just like Mom did." Jody shrugged. "He's afraid that in ten years' time I'm going to abandon my daughter."

"Hey, you're not gonna do that."

"What if I do?" Jody's blue eyes filled with fear.

I held her face in my hands, making sure her eyes were locked on mine. "You won't."

She swallowed.

Brushing my lips across hers, I tried to wipe away the look of tension marring her pretty features.

It didn't really work; her fears were still there. I couldn't help feeling like maybe they'd been buried deep all this time, and her snap earlier in the day had unlocked a dusty box of emotions hidden in her psyche.

"I still crave the stage, Leo. What if it overwhelms me one day? What if I can't be a mom anymore?"

"You can have both, Jo."

She blinked, looking unconvinced.

I smiled at her. She was so cute. "You had it the other day, singing in the studio. We can make that happen for us. I'll write, you sing. We're the perfect pair, foxy."

Her grin was delicious. I kissed it. It was impossible not to.

She shuffled around on my knee so we were facing each other, her legs either side of mine. Her fingers ran through my hair, her gaze drizzling over me like sweet honey.

"Why do you keep calling me foxy?"

A grin teased my lips as I traced one of the orange cartoon foxes on her pants. "It's these blimin' PJs."

"My pajamas?"

"Yeah," I breathed. "You're like a little sex nugget in these things. If I had my way you'd wear them all the time, just so I could keep taking them off you." I gently tugged at the tie holding her pants in place.

She giggled, her warm breath kissing my skin. "You like my foxes."

"I like my foxy lady in these foxes."

The expression in her eyes grew warm and soft. "Your foxy lady," she whispered. "I never thought

I'd get so lucky."

My lips rose at the edges.

"When you told me you'd been divorced, I figured you wouldn't be interested in another relationship, but here you are, sitting underneath me, talking like we have a future."

I pulled in a sigh, not wanting my answer to be flippant. "It's different this time around. Gerry and I left each other because it was wrong from the start."

"How do you mean?"

"She never looked at me the way you do." My eyes searched hers, my heart expanding in my chest. "I never wanted her like I want you."

"How did you get together then?"

I shrugged, giving Jody a sad smile. "I liked her, it was an instant attraction and everyone thought we were this perfect couple. We got caught up in the moment. When you've got every person you know asking you when you're gonna get married, it's hard to not believe it's the right thing to do. She never stopped to think past the wedding, and I never stopped to think past the honeymoon."

Jody's expression crumpled. "It's so easy to make mistakes, isn't it? Life-changing ones that you can't take back."

I ran my fingers into her hair and cupped the back of her head. "Life-changing ones that can lead to better things." I pulled her toward me, gently kissing her.

"Would you take it back?" she whispered. "If you could have those years over again."

I brushed my lips against her cheek, smelling her sweet scent before shaking my head. "I never would have come here if I hadn't been trying to get away. That crisis sparked something inside of me. It gave me the courage to break free and now I'm here, sitting underneath you and talking like we have a future." I grinned.

Her cheeks rose against my lips and I closed my eyes, feeling her smile.

"So, you don't mind having a future with a single mother who totally ruined her daughter's first birthday party?"

I licked my bottom lip, my smile growing. "I don't mind having a future with a girl who makes me smile every time I think about her. One who laughs at my jokes and my pig shit expressions."

Jody giggled against me and then sat back with a gasp.

"Smile!" She grinned, jumping off my lap, her pants nearly running down to her ankles. Much to my disappointment, she quickly retied them as she walked to the bookshelf. "I heard this song the other day, and I've been waiting for the perfect moment to play it to you...which this just happens to be." She picked up her phone and checked the volume on the speaker beside it before pressing play.

"Smile" by Sheppard started up.

Jody spun to face me, her white teething flashing me a jaw-dropping smile before she winked and dipped her hip, singing softly as she swayed toward me. I tried to reach for her, but she nipped out of range, jumping onto the coffee table and doing a little dance.

Her voice blended with the main singer beautifully. The sound was magic, as was the body swaying before me. It only got better when my little minx gave me a playful grin and slowly took off her shirt.

My pants grew tight instantly, my body wanting to lurch straight off the couch.

Jody wagged a finger at me, making me stay put as she unclasped her bra and threw it at me. I caught it but was too distracted by Jody's fingers as they flirted with the drawstring of her foxy pants. I threw her pink bra over my shoulder, saliva filling my mouth as my gaze lingered on her perfect breasts then started travelling down her body. Jody's grin was wicked. She did a slow spin, dropping her butt right in my face before standing up again and jumping out of my grasp. Her pants were still tied up tight, and my leg began to bob in anticipation.

Jody's tongue skimmed her lower lip, her fingers finally tugging at that string. The foxes folded together as the pants dropped to her ankles, and Jody stood before me in all her naked beauty. Raising her arms above her head, she kept swinging and swaying, her voice taking on a sexy timbre as the lyrics shifted. Her eyes hit mine when the song started talking about getting under the sheets, and I couldn't take it anymore.

Jumping up, I grabbed her against me, swinging her over my shoulder with a growl and carrying her down to the bedroom. Her melodic laughter followed in our wake and didn't cease until I dropped her onto the bed.

Her smile was sunshine and her lips were heaven as the clothes were yanked off my body and we quickly got lost beneath the sheets.

THIRTY

JODY

I could hear Angel crying, but couldn't move my butt out of bed. My body felt as useful as a plate of Jell-O. My limbs were elastic after a night of lovemaking with the oh-so-talented Leo Sinclair.

An instant grin stretched across my lips.

He was something else. I had tried to lie next to his naked body and sleep, I swear, I really had, but the sparking inferno inside me would have none of it. A loved-up high had carried me through the night, and I couldn't believe I had to face a day and actually get dressed and live like a normal person.

With a groan, I forced myself up, scrambling for

a shirt on the floor.

Angel's crying stopped.

I paused, frowning as I slid the tank top over my head. She never stopped like that. If anything, her cries grew to an all-out wail until I poked my head in the door and reminded her that Mommy hadn't abandoned her.

Jerking a look over my shoulder, I noticed the left side of the bed was empty.

He hadn't...had he?

"Good morning, Mummy," Leo sing-songed as he walked into the room with my contented one-year-old nestled in his arms.

They both stood at the edge of the bed grinning down at me, and I thought my heart was going to melt. The breath was sucked out of my lungs as Leo pressed his lips to Angel's forehead before flying her toward my arms.

"I'll go make a bottle." He kissed my cheek and left for the kitchen.

Angel snuggled her head against my chest, her fuzzy hair tickling my chin. I was struggling to find words. Not only had the hottest Australian I'd ever met spent the night in my bed, he'd also gotten my baby girl up—I patted Angel's diaper—*changed her* and was off making her morning bottle. Had I fallen into the Twilight Zone? Was I still dreaming?

"Da-ba-dah." Angel rubbed her nose against my chest, her soft little fingers wrapping around my curls.

"Did you like Leo getting you up this morning?"

"Bah-bah."

"I kind of liked it." I kissed her fuzz, unable to fight my grin. "Do you think I should let him sleep over again?"

The idea was thrilling and comforting all in the same moment. I wanted to pinch myself. I'd screwed up, made a life-changing decision that I thought would land me in no-love-city for the rest of my life, but it was happening with a really amazing guy that I still didn't think I deserved.

I nibbled my lip, a nervous chuckle escaping as I hugged my baby girl and let myself dream for the first time since I found out I was pregnant.

"Woohoo!" A shout came from the kitchen, and two seconds later Leo rushed in. His smile was so wide it took over his face. "Yes!" He started a happy dance that had me giggling.

Angel spotted her bottle in his hand and sat up, reaching for it.

Leo was too busy celebrating whatever it was to notice.

She let out a loud squawk, making him jump.

"Oh, sorry, blossom. Here you go."

She snatched it out of his hands, leaning against my chest and guzzling down the liquid. I kissed her head and smiled at her before looking back up at Leo.

"What's got you all happy dancing around my bed?"

"Aw, Jo, you're not going to believe it." He perched on the bed beside me, his eyes alight. "Bobby's contact in New York just called me. He loved the song. He's having kittens over the thing!"

"Really! Oh my gosh, that's awesome!" My squeal disrupted Angel. Her face puckered into a disapproving frown, which I made a funny face at.

Stroking her forehead, I let her get back to drinking and threw my attention onto Leo.

"So? What does that mean?"

"Well." Leo licked his bottom lip. "He's invited me to New York to perform the rest of the pieces for him and his backers. If he likes what he hears, then he'll invite me to stay and work with his team on completing the show...and then it'll hit Broadway!"

"Holy crap! That's so amazing!"

Leo grinned and planted his lips on mine. "It's happening, Jo."

"I know." I rested my hand on his chest. "And you so deserve this."

Reality nipped at my heels as the news of what he had planned really sank in.

New York.

Invited to stay.

Oh, shit, I was going to lose him!

I swallowed, forcing my lips to remain in a grin. I didn't want to ruin this moment for him. I could cry my tears later, once he'd left.

"So, um." I cleared the wobbles out of my throat. "When they buy it, will you get to be a part of producing it?"

"I don't know." Leo ran a hand through his hair. "I mean, I guess if I'm writing it they'll let me have some say, I suppose. I hope that's the case. I'd love to direct it, but I doubt they'd let me go that far."

He chuckled. "I'm sure there's some other superstar director who could do much better than me. I'll need to work my way up to that dream."

I crossed my fingers for him. Having worked with him on perfecting "I Want The World," it wasn't hard to see what a great director he could be. I would have loved to work with him one day.

But that wasn't going to happen.

Tears burned at my eyes. I distracted myself by focusing back on Angel. Her bottle was done, and she'd want food soon. Taking the bottle off her, I placed it on the bedside table and lifted her in my arms before propping her against my chest and squeezing tight.

Her soft, pudgy cheek against mine was a small comfort. At least I wouldn't be losing her to New York.

"Jo." Leo's tender voice forced me to look at him. I prayed my eyes weren't glossy. I blinked a couple of times to fool him into thinking I just had something in my eye.

His smile grew as he placed his hand on the side of my neck and gently caressed the edge of my jaw.

Shit, don't do that, Leo! I'll totally dissolve!

"I want you guys to come with me."

Okay, heart attack.

What did he just say?

"You—what?"

"I need you to perform these songs for me. Your voice for 'I Want The World' was magic. I can't imagine anyone else singing it that perfectly. You need to come and perform, and who knows where it might lead. You were born for the stage, Jo. This chance is too good to turn your back on."

"You want—but how would that—?"

"It'll work. We'll make it work. I'm due in New York at the end of June. That's plenty of time for you to learn the songs and for me to finish off the final piece."

"But what about Angel?"

"She'll come with us, of course. We can find someone to take care of her for the audition, but the rest of the time she can be there with us, and if they accept the play, then we'll set ourselves up in New York."

"New York," I whispered, my insides buzzing with a hope so strong and alluring, I wanted to burst. "You think we can do it?"

Leo chuckled. "I *know* we can. If you want something bad enough, you make it happen. I know there's risks, but if we really want this, we have to take a leap." The pads of his fingers pressed lightly against the back of my neck. His eyes searched mine, and I could see the desperate hope in his gaze as he whispered, "Do you want this?"

A slow smile grew across my lips, and I sang his lyrics, "I want the world, I want it all, ready to jump, even if I fall."

"'Cause I'm a dream chaser, which one will come true?" he sang back.

My smile grew. "New York."

"Broadway, baby."

"Broadway." I giggled and let out a squeal,

lifting Angel into the air. Her high-pitched glee made Leo and I chuckle. I threw her up and caught her against me, my eyes locking with Leo's.

"Broadway," he mouthed before giving me another kiss.

I threaded my fingers into his hair, loving the feel of his lips on mine, while my precious baby girl lightly slapped his stubbly cheek.

Capturing a dream I'd thrown to the wind was like holding a precious jewel.

I couldn't quite believe it was happening, but my brain wrapped its fingers around the idea and clung tight.

Me, on a Broadway stage.

Me, living in New York with the man I loved.

That was the life I wanted.

And now there was a chance I'd actually get it.

THIRTY-ONE

LEO

We worked our butts off over the next few weeks, fitting in practices wherever we could. We still had the building to run and a baby to raise, but we were making it happen. Jody and I were staying up late, working on songs after Angel had gone to bed. She was our alarm clock in the mornings, and we'd rush through the day, completing chores together so we could get through them quicker. Any spare time was spent practicing over at my place.

Angel would play on the floor beside us while we rehearsed, and when Jody was busy playing mum, I would tweak the pieces and finish off the orchestral arrangements.

Since Jody had agreed to come sing for me, I couldn't stop picturing her as Aria—the lead role. She would sing and dance through each of her dream worlds, finally ending up under the bright stage lights. The finale piece would start with her solo, a declaration of independent joy as she claimed her heart's true desire.

I scrubbed out my scribble with the eraser on the back of my pencil and reworked the line, playing the notes and mumbling the lyrics, trying to perfect the piece before playing it to Jody.

"Okay, we gotta go." Knocking had ceased between us. Our two apartments had become like one with a big hallway in between them. My place was for work, and Jody's was for play.

I winked at her as she stood in the entranceway, Angel on her hip and a baby bag slung over her shoulder.

"Don't stress, foxy pants. It's going to be okay." I placed my pencil down and stood from the piano stool.

"That's easy for you to say, we're not heading to your father's house right now."

Grabbing the car keys off the hook, I placed my hand on the side of her face and forced her to look at me. "He's going to be proud of you. You're heading to New York to sing on a stage. Isn't that what he wanted?"

"Yeah," she sighed. "But I'm still nervous about telling everybody."

"Well, we have to tell them today. We leave for New York next week."

"I know." She nodded.

"They'll probably be just as excited as Ella was. I wouldn't worry about it."

"Ella's the most supportive human being on the planet, she gets excited for everybody. It's Morgan I'm worried about. Miss Practicality can be a real buzz-kill when it comes to this kind of thing."

Grabbing Jody's hand, I led my two girls to the lift, humming "Dream Big" as I went.

Jody's chuckle was dry as we descended to the parking garage beneath the building, but she didn't tell me to shut up. By the time she was buckling Angel into her carseat, we were both singing the words.

Music accompanied us all the way to the Pritchett house. It helped us both fight the jitters as we made our way across town. Unfortunately, by the time we pulled into Pasadena, the music was having little effect. This was the first time I'd been to the Pritchett home, and I was going there to announce that I was taking their two youngest family members across the other side of the country and I wasn't exactly sure when we'd be back. This could go two ways—utter elation for our success or total shock. I was hoping like anything we'd get the first.

We stopped outside the front door and looked at each other.

"You ready for this?" I asked Jody as Angel struggled in my arms, stretching for the door, desperate to get inside.

Jody laughed at her daughter's antics and nodded. "Yeah, you're right, it's going to be fine. Dad will be happy that I'm pursuing this. It's what he wants."

I bent down and pressed my lips against hers. "It's what *we* want and that's the most important thing."

Her bobbing head was accompanied with a nervous smile as she opened the door and stepped inside. "Hey, everyone!"

"Hey!" The calls came from all over the house, people merging into the living area.

Morgan's grin was enormous as she lifted Angel out of my arms and greeted her niece. Sean leaned behind Morgan's shoulder and made the baby laugh with a quick game of peek-a-boo. It was kind of funny watching the enigmatic superstar act like an idiot.

Grandma Deb wrapped Jody in a hug then proceeded to squeeze the life out of me. I patted her on the back and kissed her cheek.

"Nice to see you, too, Deb." I nodded.

Jody squeezed my hand and led me to the couch. Everyone's attention was on Angel, Morgan and Grandma Deb taking turns asking Jody a bunch of questions about how she was doing. No one noticed Marshall amble in. No one except me. I felt his searing gaze on me the second he walked into the room.

I glanced up, refusing to fear the guy. From everything Jody had told me, he was being really harsh on his younger daughter. I was wise enough to know that buried hurts were probably fueling his reaction, but I was really hoping that today's news might ease the load for him a little.

"G'day, Mr. Pritchett." I rose from the couch and extended my hand.

He reluctantly took it, grunting a greeting at me.

Jody rolled her eyes when I sat down. I rubbed her back, silently reminding her to not get aggravated by her father's less-than-friendly attitude. It wouldn't matter shortly. We'd be on the other side of the country anyway.

"Dinner should be in about half an hour." Morgan bobbed Angel on her knee. "Does she need feeding first or anything?"

"No, I fed her just before we left. She'll be due for bed in a couple of hours, so dinner in thirty works well."

"Okay." Morgan's smile grew tight as she eyed her sister. Her head tipped to the side, her eyes narrowing. I felt Jody stiffen beneath my hand before Morgan asked, "What's up with you?"

"Nothing." Jody frowned.

"Oh, Jody!" Marshall spat.

Her head whipped around to look at him, her eyes wide.

"You're pregnant again, aren't you!"

Our lips parted in unison; I could see it out of the corner of my eye. A spark of anger flared through me, but Jody spoke before I could say what I really thought.

"No, Dad, I'm not! But thanks for your vote of

confidence."

He humphed, slumping back in his chair.

Jody's jaw shook as she blinked at her tears, and I couldn't just sit there and watch it happen. Threading my fingers through hers, I sat up a little straighter and looked her father right in the eye.

"Actually, we've got some really exciting news."

Morgan shot a glance at Sean before going statue-still, her neck muscles straining tight.

Jody squeezed my hand, her smile quivering when I gazed down at her.

"Leo's musical that he's been working on..." Her smile grew, pride beaming from her eyes. I winked at her, adoring the way she was looking at me. "He's been invited to audition in New York. A Broadway producer is interested in it."

"Aw, that's cool. Congratulations, man." Sean's smile was genuine. I knew he'd get it.

"So, what's that got to do with you?" Marshall's cold-water tone made me stiffen.

I looked back at him. "Jody's going to perform the songs for me. If they like what they hear, we've been invited to stay and work with a team on completing the musical and turning it into a Broadway hit."

"You're moving to New York?" Morgan's quiet question held none of the enthusiasm we were hoping for. Her long fingers gripped her niece, her face paling at the news.

"Yeah, Morgan." Jody swallowed. "It's a great opportunity."

"What about Angel?" She frowned.

"She's coming with us, of course."

"Who's going to look after her?"

"I am." Jody pointed at herself. "I only need to find care for her during the audition, and Leo's godfather knows a few families who are willing to help us out."

"You'd leave Angel with total strangers?" Marshall barked.

"Well, they're not strangers. I mean, we can trust them."

"How do you know that?"

"I—I obviously wouldn't leave her with someone I don't feel comfortable with! I'm not that bad of a mother! This is a great opportunity for me, and we can make it work. I thought you'd be happy." She pointed at her father. No one could miss the shake in her finger.

"How am I supposed to be happy about this?"

"Because I'm pursing my...dreams. I—" Jody flicked her hand in the air, letting out a disgusted scoff. "You are unbelievable!"

Marshall threw her a deadpan glare before shaking his head and rising from his seat. Hitching his pants, he walked out of the room.

Jody's face pinched tight. Shooting out of her chair, she stomped after him. I decided to stay put, figuring we'd be able to hear everything anyway.

I was right.

"I can't win with you! What do you want from me!" Jody shouted at her father.

"I want you to be happy, Jo-Jo! I want you to get everything you deserve out of this life. I don't want you to end up like your mother."

"Which is why I am chasing my dreams!"

"Yeah, to New York! With my granddaughter! Going all the way to the other side of the country with no family support. What if it doesn't work out with this guy? What are you going to do then?"

"It's going to work out, Dad."

"You barely know him!"

"I know him well enough to be in love with him."

Sean caught my eye, giving me a small congratulatory smile, but it was quickly dampened by Marshall's booming voice.

"Oh, like you were in love with the last guy? What's to say this one isn't gonna knock you up and leave you, too!"

"Leo is not like that, he'd never do that to me."

"This is a stupid idea, Jody!"

"Yeah, well, it's *my* stupid idea and I'm doing it!"

I stood from the couch the moment Jody returned. Her cheeks were flushed pink, her nostrils flaring. Storming past her grandmother, she grabbed Angel out of Morgan's hand. The baby started crying immediately, making the tension a million times worse.

"Let's get out of here," Jody snapped at me.

Lifting the baby bag onto my shoulder, I shot an apologetic smile at Grandma Deb. She waved her hand as if she'd seen it all before.

Morgan, to my surprise, didn't say a word. She sat on the couch looking shell-shocked while Sean squeezed her shoulder. His expression was glum, his eyes filling with sympathy as I followed my irate girlfriend out to the car.

Oh, man, I had a really long night on my hands.

THIRTY-TWO

JODY

I didn't talk the whole way home. I couldn't. We walked into the apartment as a subdued threesome. Angel had picked up on my mood before we even left Pasadena, crying and fussing the entire car trip. All I wanted was to settle her down and get her into bed.

I checked my watch and walked toward the bathroom. "I'm just going to bathe her."

"Sounds good," Leo murmured.

I hated that he was being so quiet. I wanted him to cheer me up, not mirror my mood! This would be the most depressing night ever if one of us didn't snap out of it!

I forced a cheery tone while I bathed my baby. She perked up a little as I splashed my fingers in the warm water. She giggled, pumping her arms up and down. I let her play in the shallow water as I leaned against the edge of the tub and watched her.

Tears scorched my eyes. I couldn't believe Dad was being such a jackass about this whole thing. His lack of faith in me stung like a hornet. He wanted me to be happy but didn't trust me enough to encourage me to make that happen for myself. How long was he going to punish me for sleeping with Stefan? Why couldn't he see how awesome Leo was? How great this opportunity was for Leo *and* me.

Water droplets hit my face and I squinted, brushing them off my cheek. Angel giggled and hit the water again. I forced a smile, tipping her nose with my wet finger. She grabbed at it, looking at me with her adoring blue eyes.

I grinned, opening my mouth and singing a soft, slow version of "I Want To Hold Your Hand," my mind wandering back to a vague memory from over a decade ago.

Dad's soft voice hummed, the sweet tune growing as we walked along the street. I brushed the reckless curls off my face, grinning up at him as he squeezed my fingers and sang, "I Want To Hold Your Hand."

We reached the crosswalk and he stopped singing.

"Daddy, why do you sing to me all the time?"

"Because I love the way your eyes light up every time you hear music. It's in your soul, just like it's in mine, and your mom's."

"Do you think I'll sound as good as her one day?"

"Oh, yeah, Jo-Jo. I think so."

"Will you guys come and watch me when I'm up on stage singing?"

"I'll be in the front row, sunshine."

And he had been...for every single one of my performances in high school. He'd beamed with pride, that low-lying sadness he lived with shut away for the night.

A tear slid down my cheek. I hurried to brush it away before Angel noticed. I was so like my mother. Would going to New York turn me into her? Would I end up leaving my baby for the stage?

"No," I whispered, determination coursing through me. I wasn't going to be like that. I was going to have both! If Mom had had the chance to pursue her dreams, she never would have left us!

I would have sat in the front row for her, and Angel could sit in the front row for me...until she was on a stage of her own.

I kept up my singing, finding the memory eerily comforting as I settled my daughter to bed. I stayed with her until her long lashes were resting on her chubby cheeks and my heart was suitably melted.

Creeping into my room, I found Leo shirtless on my bed, a sight that did completely different things to my heart. I gave him a soft smile, unable to hide the lingering sadness from my evening.

Taking off my watch, I laid it down on my bedside table.

"We don't have to go to New York."

My eyes shot to his, a frown denting my forehead. "You're not throwing away this chance, Leo. I don't care what my family says." Actually not true at all. I just didn't want to care. I ignored the disappointment trying to munch on my insides and murmured, "We'll make it work, remember?"

Moving from his spot on the bed, he came toward me, rising to his knees so our faces were aligned. "I'll look after you and Angel, Jo. I promise."

"I know." I tucked a lock of floppy hair behind his ear and ran my fingers through his stubble. I wanted to think of something cheerful to say, some way to banish my father's bitter words, but I had nothing.

Pressing my lips together, I sniffed. "I don't suppose you have a song for this situation, do you?"

A half grin pushed at Leo's lips, his eyes dancing as he reached back for his phone.

Damn, he was hot. Seeing his body stretched over my bed like that was distraction enough. Maybe I didn't need a song. The idea of using sex to drive away my sadness sounded pretty perfect.

"I have a few, actually." Leo sat back up, keeping his eyes on his phone and totally missing the fact I was pulling my clothes off and throwing them onto the floor. "Do you want something sad so you can keep crying, or do you want something to cheer you—"

His eyes caught me, rounding slightly at my near-naked form. His dopey smile was delicious as his gaze roved my body. I loved the little awe-filled smile he got on his face when he looked at me, like he'd never seen anything so beautiful.

"Don't worry about it," he croaked. "I've found the perfect song for us."

"A song for us? As in *our* song?"

"Come on, foxy pants." He tipped his head with a *get real* look that made me smile. "As if you and I could have just *one* song."

I leaned forward, pressing my breasts against his naked chest. A smile tugged at his lips, his eyes sparking with hunger as he wove his hand around my waist, his feather-light touch traveling up my spine.

"This is just a very reusable song, because it's the truth." His voice was husky as he pressed the screen and placed his phone next to my watch.

"You Make Me Happy" by Lindsey Ray started playing.

I grinned, loving the sweet sound. My hips started swaying, my insides trilling. Leo was right; this song was perfect for us. It's like the writer had read my mind, coming up with the perfect lyrics for our relationship.

Leo's eyes drank me in, the pads of his fingers skimming down my naked back. Our smiles kissed, a warm heat swimming through me as his tongue found mine. Cupping my butt, Leo flopped onto the bed, pulling me on top of him and chasing away all my sorrow with his tender kisses. His light caress sent my senses into orbit, and it was easy to believe that as long as we were together, everything would be okay.

THIRTY-THREE

JODY

In spite of all my determined talk and a lovemaking session that turned my mind to custard, I couldn't shake the fight with my dad. It plagued me, driving me insane as I fought the waves of doubt that crashed over me. The plane tickets were bought. The hotel was booked. We were *going* to NYC! I didn't care what got in the way. In three days' time, we were boarding the plane, and nothing was going to stop me.

My hands shook as I sat at Leo's piano. I squeezed my fingers together.

"Come on, you know this."

I didn't want to let Leo down, but I had been screwing up the tune for "Dream Chaser" repeatedly. It was a song in the middle between the old wise woman and the young protagonist, Aria. It was kind of her light-bulb moment in the story where she finally figures out what she wants, and when she wakes, what dream she's going to pursue.

It was a powerful song, and my voice really needed to nail that high note, making it soar right across the audition room so it pierced every soul sitting in front of me.

I could hear Angel playing in the apartment next door. I didn't usually leave her out of reach, but she was happy with her blocks, and I wanted to steal ten minutes at the piano while Leo wasn't home. I'd left both the doors open and blocked off the stairs so she could totter through to me when she was ready.

Pulling in a breath, I played the notes and sung the old lady's part first.

Dream chaser, what are you searching for?
Which door is the one that you will choose?
Dream chaser, do not be afraid
Let the music guide your heart
Hear what it will say...what it will say...

My voice crested over her note, rising in volume before Aria's solo kicked in.

I know which way to go...I think, yes,

I know where my love is leading me, I feel it
I know which way to go.
But can I get there on my own?

The keys under my fingers felt like magic as I lost myself in the song, the wise woman assuring me in her next verse that I had the strength to face any odds and that pursuing my dream and listening to my heart would secure me everything I wanted.

My smile grew as the duet picked up speed, matching the excitement growing inside of me.

I can make this dream come true
*   You can make this dream come true*
Like a light it leads me on to what I'm meant to do

You will know it in your soul
*   I will know it in my soul*
Feelings come alive and you'll know you have come home...

I've found my home
*   You've found your home*
I've found my soul
*   You found your soul*
I let the music guide...
*   Guide...*
The music guide...
*   Guide...*
I've found my home.

My voice stretched over the final note. It was a high one, and I could feel my vocal cords straining, vibrato kicking in to help see me through the note. I had to hold it for at least twelve beats, if not sixteen. It needed that time to really soar.

I finished with a triumphant huff. That time had sounded way better. I needed to get out of my own head and just focus on the music. Like the song said, if I let music guide me, I'd find home and everything I wanted.

Placing my fingers back on the keys, I decided to run through it again. I paused to listen out for Angel, but I couldn't hear anything. She wasn't crying, so I figured I had time to work through the song once more before going to check on her.

Five minutes couldn't hurt.

My fingers had stopped shaking and were working with renewed vigor the second time I played over Leo's piece. He was such a genius. The entire musical was amazing, and my insides were bubbling with pride. My broad smile was hindering my singing, but I couldn't help it. I was in love with a magical man who was going to sell his play to Broadway...and I was going to be the star of his show.

Glee bubbled within me as my voice crescendoed, but it was slashed in half by a terrifying thump and a bone-chilling scream.

I bolted off the stool, nearly tripping over as I raced out of the room and through to my apartment. Angel's wails were high-pitched and horrifying. I had come to learn her different cries, and I'd never heard anything like this before.

"Angel!" I glanced into the living area where I'd left her. The blocks were a messy pile on the floor, completely forgotten.

Surging after her sound, I screeched to a halt in the kitchen, my stomach turning as I took in the sight of my baby girl, face-first on the hard floor with blood pooling around her.

THIRTY-FOUR

JODY

"Oh shit, oh shit, oh shit!" I dropped to my knees, my arms shaking as I tried to lift Angel. Tears blurred my vision while panic clawed up my throat, making me want to wail in time with my daughter.

Blood was dripping from her face, splashing large red dots all over my shirt. With quivering fingers, I tried to figure out exactly where the blood was coming from. I touched her red-stained chin and she screamed, flinging her arms and legs.

Bile surged up my throat as I got a proper look at the large gash. Her mouth was bleeding profusely, as well. Every time she wailed, more blood-laced dribble ran out from between her lips. I was soon covered in it, the red dots merging into a large, wet stain on my shirt. Panic was starting to win, taking swift hold and turning my mind to mush. I tried to bob Angel against me and calm her down, but it wasn't working. She was hysterical...which was making me hysterical.

"Think, think." I sobbed the words, my body trembling as I begged my brain to function properly. "Stop the bleeding," I finally whispered. "Stop the bleeding," I repeated, my voice sounding a little more sure as I clung to something practical I could actually do.

Yanking open the bottom drawer, I pulled out a clean towel and pressed it against Angel's chin. This nearly sent her through the roof, but I had to stem the flow.

"I'm sorry, baby."

She grappled with me, scratching at my hands with her little nails while I scrambled for my phone.

Leo's number popped up first. I dialed it and paced impatiently.

No answer.

"What the—Are you kidding me!" Who the hell didn't have their phones on them at ALL TIMES! What was the point of having one if you weren't going to answer it!

I nearly threw the device across the room. Last-minute logic stopped me from killing my only form of communication.

Leo had the car with Angel's baby seat in it. I knew I had to get her to a doctor, but how?

"Ambulance?" My fingers shook as I went to dial, but my phone vibrated and started ringing.

I saw Dad's number and didn't hesitate. Arguments be damned, I needed him.

"Dad," I answered with a wail, my voice breaking apart as I joined my daughter in an all-out cry-fest.

"Jody? What's the matter?"

"Angel's hurt and I don't know what to do. There's blood everywhere." I had to practically shout to be heard over her screaming.

"I'm on my way." His voice was clipped but calm, and I needed that right now.

"Do I call an ambulance?"

"What are her injuries?"

"Split chin and maybe a cut in her mouth. I'm not sure, she won't let me look at it."

"Okay, don't panic. She's conscious and breathing. I'm ten minutes away. Just sit tight and I'll drive you guys to the emergency room."

I nodded, my head bobbing like a jackhammer as he hung up.

Sucking in a breath, I sat Angel down on the island.

"It's okay, baby. I know it hurts, but Grandpa's coming, okay? He's going to look after us."

My shaking voice didn't calm her. She batted at my hands, still trying to pull the towel off her face. I gave in to her request but changed my mind when I noticed the wide gash on her chin was still oozing.

I lifted her into my arms, squeezing my eyes against her screams.

"Shhhh, it's okay. It's okay." I kept whispering the words, my body swaying back and forth. I nearly stepped in the blood on the floor, my forehead creasing as I tried to figure out what she'd done.

The cupboard doors beneath the sink were flung open. It didn't take me long to work out that she must have climbed up the shelving and gotten up to the countertop before slipping and...

"I should have been watching you." My voice squeaked. "I shouldn't have left. I'm so sorry, baby."

I kept on muttering apologies between hiccupping sobs.

I didn't even hear Dad walk in.

"Jody?" He came up behind me.

I jolted, spinning to face him. He took in the blood-soaked towel against Angel's face and his expression morphed with horror.

"What happened?" He lurched toward us.

"I think she was climbing and she fell."

"You think? You weren't watching her?"

"Of course I wasn't! Do you think I would have let her climb onto the counter if I had been!"

"She's one! You should be with her at all times. How did she get up there in the first place?"

I looked to the ceiling, fresh tears filling my eyes as I listened to Dad's reprimand. I knew he was right. I didn't need him to spell it out for me.

"I screwed up, okay! Come on, that's what you're used to now, right?"

His face crested with sorrow.

I ignored it, my volume increasing with Angel's cries. "But it doesn't change the fact that my baby girl is in pain and I need to help her! HELP ME!" I screamed.

Raising his hands in surrender, I didn't miss the apology swamping his expression as he came around behind me and laid a hand on my back. "It's okay, Jo-Jo. I'm here." He kissed the side of my face. "It's gonna be okay."

*****

Dad didn't have a baby seat in his truck, so I sat Angel in my lap in the backseat and prayed she wouldn't have to endure two accidents in one day. Guilt was a heavy burden, weighing me down and causing fresh waves of tears to swamp me every few minutes. Dad drove at a quick clip, but I never felt unsafe. We pulled into the hospital parking lot and Dad ushered us through the emergency room doors where a nurse dealt with us swiftly.

Within twenty minutes, Angel was seen by a tender, sweet doctor who reminded me of Sean's brother, Kip. He was tall and lean, his long, dark fingers precise as he stitched Angel's gash. His low, soft voice comforted Angel, even when he was trying to inject an anesthetic into her chin. Once she was calm, he examined her mouth and pointed out where she'd bitten her tongue.

"Those things bleed pretty bad, but they also heal quickly."

"Is she going to be okay?" I wrapped my arms around myself.

"Of course she is." He smiled, rubbing her back gently. "But she did fall and hit her face, so I'd like to keep her overnight, just to monitor her and make sure there are no hidden injuries lurking where we can't see 'em."

"Okay," I whispered, feeling sick as I tried to smile at my baby girl.

Her blue eyes were so forgiving. I didn't deserve those chubby arms reaching out for me.

"Uh, you'll need to fill out some paperwork, and I'm sorry, standard procedure, but someone from Child Services is going to want to chat to you."

"Child Services?" I frowned.

"We just need to be sure that the baby is in a safe environment."

My stomach dropped as I cradled Angel against me.

"I would never hurt my baby."

The doctor's brown eyes softened with a kind smile. "I can see that, but it's protocol. I'm sure you'll have nothing to worry about."

I nodded, feeling numb as I followed the doctor out to the waiting room.

As soon as Dad saw us, he lurched from his chair and came forward with outstretched arms. Another wave of tears crested over me. I seriously didn't know what I would have done if he hadn't been there for Angel and me.

THIRTY-FIVE

JODY

The Child Services interview was brutal. She questioned me on everything, not letting up until she was sure I wasn't abusing my daughter. It didn't stop her from making me feel like a piece of dirt for leaving Angel unchecked for so long, though.

"I realize being a single mother is hard work. It's tiring and relentless, but you cannot afford to put your child at risk like this again. If you're struggling, you need to get yourself some support."

I nodded, fear curling through me at the idea of leaving my family support network and flying to the other side of the country. What if Angel fell in New York? Who would I call to help me? If Leo was out of reach, I'd be all alone.

"Who brought you to the emergency room today?"

"My father," I croaked, my forehead crinkling. Why had he been calling me?

"Good, I'm glad you have family close by. Use them, get their help. Most are more than willing if you'll just ask."

I nodded again, unable to meet her stern gaze.

"Jody, from what Doctor Johnson told me, you obviously love your daughter. I can see you're young and she probably wasn't planned, but you've chosen to keep her, and you need to take that seriously. Children must come first until they are able to look after themselves."

Her eyebrow peaked high, reminding me of my strict math teacher from twelfth grade. Man, I'd hated her.

The social worker's words drove into me, feeling like nettles. My conscience burned, charring my insides and making me feel ill. If I hadn't been lost in the song, the music... If I hadn't let my yearning for the stage take hold, Angel never would have gotten hurt.

"I'll never play the piano again, I swear."

"That's a little drastic." She sniffed out a dry laugh. "Look, we all know accidents happen, but you do need to ask yourself what you could have done differently to avoid this one." The lady patted my arm, her stern reprimand giving way to a sympathetic smile.

"I know exactly what I could have done differently." I shook my head, loathing myself, right down to my core.

She rose from her chair and I followed suit, tugging my bloodstained shirt straight.

"I won't ever let it happen again."

"I feel confident of that." She hugged her paperwork to her chest, her smile growing with warmth.

My lips wobbled when I tried to smile back.

"Go and see your baby. I've arranged to have a bed set up in the room so you can stay with her for the night."

"Thank you."

She opened the door for me, and I listened to the squeak of my shoes on the hospital floor as I made my way up to Angel's room. Dad had stayed with her, much to my relief. I hadn't wanted him sitting in on my shameful interview. The fact I'd even had to have it made me want to curl into a ball and die.

Popping out from the elevator, I slowed my pace, checking room numbers as I followed the directions I'd been given. The pediatrics floor was filled with sounds of crying babies and bustling nurses. I made my way down to the end of the corridor and found Angel's room.

Peeking my head inside, I swallowed back my greeting, too enraptured by the sight before me to speak. Ella and Morgan were leaning against the hospital bed, holding hands and watching my dad.

He was holding Angel, kissing the tips of her

fingers as he gently swayed around the room singing, "The Way You Do The Things You Do." She gazed up at him, her blue eyes sparkling in spite of the deep bruise marring her milky skin.

A rush of memories came flooding over me, Dad humming to me as we walked down the street or danced around the kitchen doing the dishes.

I sucked in a breath, my face bunching. Whenever he'd sung to me like that, I knew without a doubt that he loved me—I'd felt it in my soul.

And there he was, singing to Angel while my sister and best friend sat waiting for me...waiting to wrap me in their arms and tell me everything would be okay. Waiting to assure me that I was still a good person and they loved me, no matter what I did.

They loved me.

And Dad, he loved my baby girl.

Watching them dance together filled me with such a sense of...

"Home," I whispered.

Closing my eyes, I felt the tears cascading over my cheeks. I knew what I had to do. I knew what my heart was telling me, and all of a sudden it hurt to breathe.

THIRTY-SIX

LEO

I pressed the lift button three times, eager to get upstairs. I'd had such a brilliant day and couldn't wait to tell Jody all about it. Thanks to Bobby's contact and his genius sound tech, I now had the full compositions for "I Want the World" and "Dream Chaser" finished. He'd helped me tweak the finer details, and I'd been able to hand over a full score of music for both those songs. I wanted to be as prepared for the audition as possible. I knew they would want to make changes, but I figured the more prepared I was, the more professional I'd look and the greater the chance of actually getting a say in how this musical was presented.

Pulling out my phone, I checked the screen, realizing I'd totally forgotten about it. I'd missed a call from Jody but was about to walk through her door anyway.

With a grin, I slide the phone away and walked straight into her place.

"Jo, you're not going to believe my day. Sorry I missed your call, but—"

My voice cut short when I looked up and found Marshall in the kitchen with a mop in his hand. He was wearing his usual grumpy expression, and it instantly made me uneasy.

"Hi, Mr. Pritchett. Um, where's Jody?"

His lips pursed, his brown gaze still drilling into me. I gripped the door handle.

"She's at the hospital," he finally muttered.

Fear ripped through me. "What?"

He didn't say more, just turned back to his mopping. Lurching into the apartment, I came around the kitchen counter, ready to grab his shirt and demand he tell me more, but then I saw the red, watery marks on the floor, and my anger was railroaded by a sickening terror.

"Oh, shit, what happened?" My mind jumped to all sorts of nasty conclusions, making it hard to see straight. The last time I'd felt this scared, I'd been listening to Deb on the phone; she was crying and telling me my brother had just had a heart attack.

Marshall wouldn't meet my horrified gaze, just kept washing away the blood.

"Tell me she's okay." My voice shook. I sucked

in a ragged breath and he looked up at me, his expression softening with surprise.

"You're really worried about her?"

"Of course I bloody am!" I yanked the beanie off my head, tempting to throw it at him. This guy was unbelievable! "You're mopping blood off her kitchen floor!"

I felt sick. Leaning over, I rested my hands against my knees, gasping in mouthfuls of air in an attempt to regulate my heartbeat. "Look, mate, I know you don't like me, but I really couldn't give a flying fuck right now." I stood tall, my shaking voice stealing my thunder. "I love your daughter...and your granddaughter! Now, tell me where the hell they are!"

Marshall swallowed, gripping the mop in his hand and pulling in a slow sigh. "Angel had a fall today."

"Angel," I whispered the word, a newfound panic sizzling in my gut. Tears glassed over my eyes before I could even stop them. Not my sweet little girl. "How bad is it?"

I didn't want to hear the answer, but at the same time, I *needed* to know.

"She cut her chin open and bit her tongue. She's in the hospital overnight. Jody's with her."

I pulled on my beanie and was walking for the door before he'd even finished. "Where? Which hospital!"

Pausing at the door, I spun to face him, desperation making my movements emphatic.

Marshall's hesitation made me want to rip his

bloody head off.

"Please!" I thumped the door, making it swing open and smack against the doorstop.

He looked to the floor, a slow smile forming on his lips as he nodded...and then gave me detailed directions.

*****

Visiting hours were over, but I lied my way through, claiming I was Angel's father. The nurse at reception bought my lie easily, probably because I said it with such conviction. I loved that little girl like she was my own, and the idea of her going through trauma near killed me.

The lift moved like a grandpa snail but finally pinged open on the fourth floor. I raced down to the right room, slowing to catch my breath when I spotted Jody in the chair beside Angel's cot, holding her daughter's little fingers through the bars. She looked ready to shatter.

"Hey," I whispered, stepping softly into the room so as not to disturb the other patient behind the curtain.

Jody's smile was sad, her eyes glistening as I stopped at the end of the bed.

"Hey, Leo." Ella smiled up at me from the other side. She was obviously tired, but it did nothing to hinder the sweet expression on her face.

I gave her a little nod of recognition.

Clearing her throat softly, she stood from her chair. "I'm gonna go and get some coffee."

"No." Jody shook her head. "Ella, go home.

Angel's asleep now and I'm okay."

"Are you sure?"

"Yes. Thank you for staying for so long."

"Of course, Jo-Jo. I'm always here for you." She moved around me, placing a kiss on the top of Jo's head before squeezing my arm and leaving.

My sigh was slow and heavy as I gazed into the cot. Angel's chin was bandaged up, but it didn't hide the purple bruising around her mouth. My gut twisted in agony, feeling her pain as if it were my own.

"Geez, Jo, I'm so sorry I wasn't there today. I didn't even hear my phone ring."

She shook her head, her lips forming a wobbly line as she blinked at fresh tears.

I moved to her side, rubbing the back of her neck and crouching down beside her. "You doing okay?"

Her teeth pinched her lips together. Shaking her head, she turned away from me.

"Hey," I whispered, resting my forehead against her cheek. "She's okay."

"I should have been watching her."

"Accidents happen."

"This one didn't have to. I was careless. I left her playing in the living room while I practiced at your piano. I'd blocked off the stairs and left the doors open, but..." She shook her head. "It wasn't good enough. I screwed up."

"Jo, you can't be too hard on yourself. You—"

"Stop." Her eyes hit mine, blue and vibrant, even in the dim lamplight. "I was wrong today, don't try and tone it down. My daughter ended up in the hospital and has stitches in her face, because I left her for too long." She licked at the tear running down the edge of her mouth, her gaze shifting back to Angel's face. "We can't go with you to New York, Leo."

"What?" My face bunched with a frown.

Her curls rustled over her shoulders as her head shook yet again. "I couldn't reach you today, and my dad ended up taking us to the hospital. I can't move to the other side of the country to pursue a dream that will put Angel at risk."

I licked my bottom lip, telling myself to think about where she was coming from, but I couldn't. She was being illogical, letting her tattered emotions rule this decision.

"Jo, this was a one-off freak accident. It'll probably never happen again."

"But what if it does, or something else?" She sucked in a quick breath. "I need my family around me, Leo. I need the support. I made the decision to keep her. I can't just run off and start pursuing the stage and forget that I have a one-year-old I'm responsible for."

"We'll find care for her in New York. We'll make it work."

"Would you stop saying that!" She slapped her leg, finally turning to face me properly. "What if we can't make it work?"

I opened my mouth, but she cut me off before I could speak.

"I know what it's like to be abandoned and yes,

Angel is only one, but I would rather die than have her go through what I did. I want her to know without a doubt that her mommy loves her and that she's more important than anything. I can't pursue the stage right now, Leo. Angel needs me to be her mother and that's it. I have to think about what's best for her...and moving miles away from people who love and support me is not what's best for her!"

I picked up Jody's fingers, squeezing them between mine as I tried to bring my raging emotions into check. Damn, it hurt. I didn't want to give up New York, but there was no way I'd be able to change Jody's mind after an argument like that.

"Okay," I sighed. "Okay, so I'll shop the musical around here then. There's bound to be someone in LA who'll be interested, right?"

"Leo, you can't." She rubbed her thumb over my knuckles. "You have to go and take this chance."

"I don't want to go to New York without you."

"You have to. This is what you want. This is what you've been working so hard for."

"But I love you, Jo."

Her expression folded, her lips trembling as she sucked in a breath. "I love you, too, which is why I have to let you do this." Pulling her hand free of my grasp, she swiped at her tears. "I'll feel guilty for the rest of my life if I hold you back. This is why you came to the States. This is everything you want."

"Not everything," I mumbled.

"Leo, you'll regret it. If you pass this up, you'll regret it, and I don't want that to hinder us. I don't want it to be something that you'll hold against me on some subconscious level. You *have* to go."

"No, actually, I don't. It's my decision."

Jody's face bunched with a mixture of agony and frustration. "You don't know what you're saying! You don't know what it's like to have a dream ripped out of your hands. I don't want that for you."

"I don't want to do this without you!" My voice was growing tight and strained. Did she honestly not get it?

"You are going!"

My eyes narrowed; I couldn't help glaring at her just a little. My hackles rose whenever anybody ordered me around like that. "And what if I stay?"

"Then we're through. I'm not letting you give everything up for me." Crossing her arms she slumped back in her chair and wouldn't look my way.

Damn if that didn't rip me in half.

I wanted to stand up and yell in her face, tell her she couldn't boss me around, but I couldn't bring myself to do it, because what if she was right?

Unable to speak past that thick swell of emotion in my throat, I leaned forward and took her face between my hands, rubbing my thumb gently across her lips. They trembled beneath my touch, and I placed my lips against them. She kissed me back, her body quivering.

When I pulled away, she wrapped her arms

around my neck, squeezing until I thought the circulation might be cut off. I gripped her to me, never wanting to let go. A new argument for New York formed on my lips, but I couldn't make it.

In that moment, it didn't matter if I thought we could overcome the odds, she didn't...and I could tell that nothing I said or did would convince her otherwise.

She was staying to be the best mother she could be.

I left about an hour later. We didn't say much to each other, just sat and watched Angel sleeping. I drove home in a daze and arrived back to an empty, soulless apartment. Marshall had left Jody's place; I could tell by the lack of light coming from under the door.

Slamming my own door shut behind me, I leaned against the wood, feeling like a tattered wreck. All the excitement of my journey across the country had been shattered by Angel's accident and Jody's decision.

Throwing my keys on the counter, I headed for the piano.

My rough sheet music for "Dream Chaser" was still on the stand. Jody must have been working on that one. She knew how much I wanted it to shine. She'd been working for me.

Damn, I wanted her to sing it so bad.

Ripping off my beanie, I threw it over my shoulder and slumped onto the stool. The keys let out a disjointed groan as I leaned my elbows against the keyboard and rested my head in my palms.

It wouldn't be the same without her.

She turned my dream into sunlight. She made it bigger, better, more perfect. She enhanced every note, every beat...she made it everything I couldn't on my own.

Jerking back in my seat, I placed my fingers on the keys and played an E-flat chord, my fingers fiddling with it as I tested out a few variations and chord combos. Closing my eyes, I let my fingers take control, ridding my body of the myriad of emotions. They swirled into the room, a cacophony of sounds that slowly started to take shape and become a mournful tune...a pointless argument that could not be resolved...an everything dream that was no longer coming true.

THIRTY-SEVEN

JODY

Angel was discharged by nine o'clock the next morning. Morgan drove my tired ass home and put both Angel and me down for a nap the second we walked in the door. When I woke to Angel's cries, I hauled my butt out of bed and collected her up. She was still pretty sensitive and fragile. I made sure to give her extra cuddles and attention as I went about the day.

She fed okay but couldn't play on her own, needing my attention basically twenty-four-seven. I had no idea where Leo was. He hadn't popped over, and I didn't have the strength to go and knock on his door. I'd seen his face when I told him we weren't coming to New York.

If only he knew how much it was killing me, too, but I couldn't let that show. He had to go. He had to take this chance. He wanted Broadway more than anything, and he was a good enough guy to give that up just to keep me happy. Well, I wasn't having it.

I loved him enough to send him across the country so he could get everything he'd ever dreamed of.

My fingers tapped on the kitchen counter as I held Angel on my hip and looked around the apartment. It was going to be so lonely without him. So quiet. So depressing.

The phone rang, snapping me out of my stupor. I picked it up and noticed Ms. Thornby's name flashing on the caller ID. I closed my eyes with a sigh. I had no idea what she wanted, but I did know that I couldn't handle it. I didn't want to hear her complaints or try to figure out how to solve them. Placing the phone on the counter, I let the call go through to voicemail.

I turned to Angel, twisting one of her soft curls gently around my finger. "Hey, do you want to move back in with Grandpa?"

She looked at me with those big blue eyes of hers and said, "Ba-ba."

I grinned, kissing her nose. "Yeah, it's a good idea, isn't it?"

He'd offered it to me that morning, when he'd called to check in. I was busy trying to sign Angel's paperwork, so had rushed through the conversation, telling him I'd think about it...and I had...all day.

It was time to go home.

The phone started ringing again. Pulling in a slow, defeated sigh, I ignored it and walked Angel through to my room.

"Time to get packing." I forced a cheery note that I'm sure even my one-year-old could see through. She was gracious enough not to let me know as I sat her down in the middle of my bed and pulled out a suitcase.

*****

I lugged the second suitcase over to the door. Sean and Morgan were due to arrive in the next hour or so. I had everything except Angel's crib and changing table packed up. The rest of the furniture had come with the house, so it was a pretty easy move. If Leo was okay with it, I'd come back for the table and crib the next day when I could borrow Dad's truck. She'd sleep in the little portable crib for the night, which Morgan said she'd set up before she came to collect me.

I fought tears the entire afternoon. Angel ended up falling asleep on my bed, making the second half of packing a million times faster. I still had no idea where Leo was and felt bad I was leaving without even telling him. I knew I was shirking my responsibility, but he'd already arranged for someone else to take over the care of the building while we were in New York. They were moving into Leo's apartment the next day.

My face puckered. We'd had it all planned so perfectly. He'd walk in, we'd walk out and fly to NYC.

I rubbed the heel of my hand between my breasts, trying to dull the ache.

A soft knock at the door made me flinch. Angel crawled toward me and used my pants to help her stand. I picked her up and moved to the door.

"Please don't be Ms. Thornby," I murmured.

The second I opened the door, Angel squealed and stretched out, wriggling her fingers and begging our visitor to take her. My smile was sad as I handed her to Leo, who gently nestled her against him.

"Hey, cherry blossom." He kissed her forehead and ran his finger down her pudgy little cheek. She nestled her head against his shoulder and wrapped her arms around his neck.

He gazed at me, his green eyes begging me to reconsider.

I bit my lips together and looked to the floor, kicking at the corner of my suitcase.

"Where are you going?" His voice sounded kind of lifeless.

I couldn't look at him. Crossing my arms, I shrugged. "Back home. I figured what's the point of staying when you won't be here."

"They might not take it. I might be back by tomorrow night."

"Leo." My chuckle was soft and shaky. "You

wrote it...of course they'll take it."

"I wrote it for you," he murmured.

My head shot up, my gaze colliding with his. The sad smile dancing within them melted me. I couldn't breathe as he stared down at me, his lips forming that little half grin of his. Holy heartbeat, I was going to miss that face.

Without a word, he unzipped the satchel sitting across his shoulders and, one-handed, wrestled a thick wad of paper out. It was tied with a red ribbon.

I took it off him and shifted the ribbon aside to read.

Dream Chaser

A musical by Leo Sinclair

"I know you're going to shake your head at this, but it was Jody inspired. It all started that day I saw you singing 'Defying Gravity' in this kitchen." He pointed to the spot I'd stood with my arms outstretched, blissfully unaware of his eyes on me.

"I was your muse?"

"For every song." His voice cracked.

I gripped the musical in my hand, running my thumb lightly over the cover page. I held gold. Leo gold—the most precious gift anyone had ever given me.

"I know you haven't heard the whole thing in order yet, so I wanted you to have a full copy, including the alternate ending."

"Why did you need an alternate? The one you have now is so perfect."

"Is it?" His wistful question was broken, the heartache cresting over his face enough to fold me in half.

I pinched my lips together, refusing to utter the words I so desperately wanted to say.

All I could do was stare at those beautiful green eyes of his. They were telling me so much. I knew he had a song for this moment, but I was too scared to ask what it was. Knowing would make me cry, and I was scared that if I started now, I'd never stop.

The elevator doors pinged open and Morgan and Sean appeared behind Leo, breaking our spell. Angel grinned at her aunt and uncle while I rubbed a hand over my face and tried to be brave.

"Hey, guys." Sean nodded at us both. With an understanding smile, he lifted the two suitcases at my feet.

"C'mere, you." Morgan grinned, holding out her hands for Angel.

She shook her head, clinging to Leo.

"I'll carry her down to the car if you like." Leo's voice cracked.

Morgan nodded, her expression sorrowful as she stepped toward me and wrapped her arm around my shoulders. I squeezed her back, but quickly pulled away before I lost it. Grabbing up Angel's box of toys, I handed them to Morgan and then flung the diaper bag and my purse over my shoulders before hugging the musical to my chest.

When we reached the car, Leo had already buckled Angel in and was kissing her little knuckles goodbye. He closed the door as I approached, taking the things off me and gently laying them in the trunk. Sean and Morgan got into the car. I crossed my arms in time with the clicking doors and leaned my butt against the car.

"Well, have a safe trip and let me know how it goes."

"I will." Leo rubbed my arms, stepping into my space and kissing the top of my head.

Unable to resist, I wrapped my arms around him, pressing my forehead against his cheek, breathing in his scent. "I'm going to miss you."

"I'll come back whenever I can."

"Okay." I nodded.

He pulled back, holding my face in his hands. "I love you, foxy pants."

He kissed me before I could say it back, his hot mouth making my knees weak. My head spun as I clung to him, holding it all in.

After a few scorching moments, he let me go and stepped back, jerking onto the sidewalk and crossing his arms. I got into the car and slammed the door behind me, gripping my elbows as if that would somehow diminish the aching pain.

I swallowed, locking the tears inside.

"Let's go, Sean," Morgan whispered.

As he pulled away, Angel sat up in her seat and started waving. "Ba-bye, we-O."

Her soft voice undid me.

MELISSA PEARL

Slapping my hands over my face, I bent in my seat and quietly sobbed as I let go of a dream I never deserved. A fleeting moment in time that was pure magic and I knew, down to my core, I'd never have again.

THIRTY-EIGHT

LEO

The rest of my night was total shit. I tried to pack for New York, but my mind was numb and fuzzy. I threw in the clothes I thought I might need, but wasn't really sure. I had my laptop, my music, and the full score—all the things I *really* needed. I ran through the songs again, hating that I was the one who had to sing them all now. I could do it, but I'd never sound as beautiful as Jody.

I got to the alternate ending, wondering if I'd even sing it for them. It had consumed me over the past twenty-four hours, an ear-worm that wouldn't let up. My mournful E-flat melody had become something else entirely. I should never have written the bloody thing—it was throwing me into total turmoil. It just came out, though, like somehow it needed to be written. A pure, true song that said everything I couldn't...everything illogical inside of me.

I forced myself to play through it, but my enthusiasm waned and I didn't even get to the end of the first chorus. I jumped away from the piano, walking around my apartment in morose silence. I didn't even want to listen to music. There were no songs for my moment, just this low-lying despair. I'd felt it before, when things were falling apart with Gerry. Although, somehow this time seemed worse.

With Gerry, I felt bad that I'd be letting people down.

This time, I felt hollow.

A ringing phone woke me at ten the next morning.

"Yeah?" I mumbled into the device.

"Hey, little brother."

"Aw, hey, Kev. How's it going, mate?"

"Just wanted to wish you luck."

"Oh, yeah."

"Your plane leaves this afternoon, right?"

"Yep." I sat up, running fingers through my tousled hair and rubbing at my blurry eyes.

"So, why don't you sound more excited?"

I groaned, flopping my head back on the couch and filling him in. He listened quietly, umming and ahhing appropriately. Typical Kev.

"So, I'm flying solo and it, uh, sucks. It's kind of hard to get excited." I squeezed my eyes shut. "I mean, I know going is the right thing to do. I've passed up my dreams for a woman before, and look where that got me. Logically, leaving her and a kid who isn't even mine makes all the sense in the world!" I slapped my hand against the arm of the couch. "I'll regret it if I don't do this. She's right to make me leave and pursue this. It just shows how much she loves me."

"Yeah, it does sound like she loves you."

I sighed, my head drooping forward. "Then why is she telling me to leave her?"

Kev laughed. "What did you want her to tell you? Stay?"

"Yeah, maybe. I don't know!" I scratched at my stubble. "If she did, would I resent her for it?"

"Sounds like the decision comes down to you, mate."

"I don't know what to do."

"What's your heart telling you?"

"Both!" I pushed myself off the couch and started pacing. "That's what's killing me. I *want* both!"

"We can't have it all, little brother."

I gritted my teeth.

"Listen, why don't you at least go to New York, do the audition, chat with the guys, and you can make your decision after that."

"Yeah, yeah. That's sensible and all that, but..."

"But what?"

I sighed. "I guess I'm just scared if I do, that I'll

287

get caught up and never make it back."

"Well, then you need to ask yourself what you want more. I don't know this girl, but is she worth sacrificing your ultimate dream for? You want Broadway, mate. That's why you left Aussie, so you could go and see your work on a big, bright stage. To hear that audience cheering for something you've created. That's what you wanted, remember?"

"Yeah, I remember."

"I want you to get to the end of your life and have no regrets. You deserve this, Leo. You've got more talent in your little toe than half of us wankers. Don't waste it because you're cruising on a love-high right now."

"But you and Deb, I mean, you guys are still in love, right?"

I heard the smile in Kev's voice. "Mate, she's my ray of sunshine, but it's not always easy."

"Do you ever regret marrying her?"

"Never. When you know, you know...you know?"

I grinned. "Yeah, mate."

"If this Jody girl's the one, she'll still be waiting for you when you get back."

They were comforting words. It took the edge off a little, made it easier to finish my packing, but they didn't take away the ache, or that niggle of uncertainty as I slammed the cab door closed and said, "LAX, please."

THIRTY-NINE

JODY

Angel had an awful night. The pain in her chin stopped her from sleeping, and the fact her mother was a crying mess probably didn't help either. I hated being back in my old bed. I missed Leo. I missed my little apartment. Dad had been nice to me since I'd returned, talking gently as he helped us settle in. Morgan and Sean had hung around until I was falling asleep in the armchair. They left shortly after dark, and I went to bed only to be woken by Angel within the hour.

The day was total shit.

Angel was all out of kilter, and I cried my way

through unpacking. I still had to go and collect Angel's crib and changing table, but I didn't have the guts. I couldn't see Leo again, and so I spent the day waiting until I knew he'd left for the airport.

It was slow-going. The minutes ticked by like hours. The musical he'd written for me sat on the edge of my desk, calling me. I tried to ignore it, but by midday, I had to give in.

Angel went down for a second nap to try to catch up. Dad had popped out, and so I took the chance to sit at the piano and lose myself in *Dream Chaser*.

It was a beautiful play. Seeing it in order made me realize that Leo had written it for me. I sight-read the songs I didn't know so well, sung with gusto the ones I knew by heart, and then I reached the end and found a new song...the alternate ending Leo had come up with last-minute.

The girl, Aria, has captured her dream. A life of song and music, of color and stage lights. She's certain. The colorful, explosive moment wakes her from slumber, breaking her fever, but as she sits up, she finds the boy she once loved sitting on the end of her bed, vigilantly waiting for her to awaken.

Aria looks at Franco, confused at first.

Franco was a dream she walked away from at the beginning of the second act. She was afraid by the prospect of possibly losing him, or him straying, or something taking him out of her life.

Even though he made her happy, she decided the risk was too high. She knew she needed a dream that was hers alone, a dream that would fulfill her completely so she didn't have to rely on anybody else.

"Leo, what did you do?" I whispered.

Franco doesn't say a word, but opens his arms, a willing lover.
This is Aria's final choice.
A slow smile forms on her lips and she starts to sing.

Running my fingers over the score, I mouthed the title of the song, "My Everything Dream."

Finding middle C, I pressed the note repeatedly as I skimmed over the music, and then my fingers found their position and I began to play the melody.

I thought I knew. I thought my heart had told me so.
I'd found my home. I was so certain.
I thought my plan was foolproof, nothing could go wrong
But now I've found, more than the music.

And I've learned a whole new thing.
That dreams can shift and change
And with certainty, now I can finally say.

It is you.
You're my everything dream.

More than lights, more than song, you're my heartbeat
It is you
You're the one that I need
You are the sun, you are my life, my everything

My voice caught on the final note, my eyes blurring with tears. She chose him. She changed her mind so they could be together.

"What the hell are you trying to say, Leo?" I hit the keys, the disjointed sound making me cringe.

"You okay?" Morgan's soft question made me gasp. I spun in my seat and saw my sister leaning against the doorframe.

"How long have you been standing there?"

Morgan gave me a sheepish grin. "Long enough to know that's a beautiful song."

My shoulders slumped. "It's Broadway, Morgan. He's been working so hard for this. It's his dream come true. I'm not going to take that away from him. It's everything he wants."

"By the sounds of that song, maybe it's not." Morgan pointed at the music behind me, stepping into the room and perching on the arm of the couch.

"He doesn't know what he's saying! He doesn't know what it's like to give up something you've wanted your whole life."

"He doesn't have to give it up. He can still have his musical. He just wants you to be part of it."

"I can't move to New York, Morgan!" My eyes shot up the stairs, thinking of my precious baby, injured thanks to me.

Morgan grasped my wrist. "Would you stop blaming yourself? You could have been sitting on the toilet when that happened."

"But I wasn't. I was sitting at a piano, getting lost like I always do. Music always gets me in trouble."

"It also brings you to life." Morgan tutted, shaking her head. "I know you hate being compared to Mom, but you are like her. She was always happiest when she was singing, but she never let herself do it, because instead of making her happy, it just made her feel like she was missing out. So she sacrificed everything she was passionate about to raise us, and then she imploded and took off. You don't want to do that to Angel."

"I never would! And yes, I do hate being compared to Mom, thank you very much!"

Morgan grinned, gathering up my fingers in her own. "So don't be like her then. Let yourself sing. Let your passion shine. You were born to be on a stage and yes, you're a mother and it does make things more difficult, but it doesn't make them impossible. You have to make sure you're getting the things you need, too, and ultimately, Angel will be happier for it."

"Happy mommy, happy kid."

"Pretty much." Morgan chuckled, touching my face. "You may not get Broadway stage lights on you, but you can still sing and you can *love*."

"I can't steal his dreams just to make my own come true."

Morgan frowned, pointing over my shoulder and saying, "It is you. You're my everything dream, more than lights, more than song, you're my heartbeat. It is you, you're the one that I need. You are the sun, you are my life, my everything." She pursed her lips. "Sounds to me like you guys might be each other's dreams."

"Then why is he going to New York!" I threw my hands in the air.

"Because you told him he had to! You basically said you'd break up with him if he didn't go."

"Because I *know* he wants this."

"Jo-Jo, I think he wants you more."

I dropped my head into my hands with a small scream. "But he deserves that stage, the accolades, the applause."

"Correct me if I'm wrong, but I've heard that people clap in LA, too." Morgan's dry voice made my head pop up. "It could just be a rumor, of course." She winked.

I slapped her arm with a little snort, my face crumpling. "He wants Broadway. He deserves it."

"Then go and have it with him."

"Hello! I have a one-year-old! Dad's right, I can't just leave my family and move over there."

"Why not? You can make it work somehow. The least you could do is be there for the audition. You can work out the details later."

A disbelieving laugh punched out of my chest. "My baby is sleeping upstairs, and you're telling me to go and jump on a plane to New York?"

"The audition's tomorrow, right? I can look after

Angel until then, and you can fly straight back. If they accept, we work out the details, and we get you over there somehow. At least you'd be with Leo."

The idea sounded phenomenal and scary at the same time. My insides skittered with doubts, nerves, excitement. "I can't have everything I want, Morgan."

"Okay, fine." Morgan leaned toward me. "Then what do you *need*?"

I couldn't breathe. There was one only word lodged in my throat.

Morgan was right; I didn't have all the details worked out, but I knew what my everything dream was. A three-letter word that I'd basically ordered out of my life.

"Call him. Tell him you've changed your mind."
I bit my lip.
"Jody, call him!"

Pulling out my phone, I unlocked the screen and found his number. Holding my breath, I pressed the red dial button and raised it to my ear.

It went straight to voicemail.

I hung up before leaving a message. "It's either off or he's on the other line."

Morgan checked her watch. "What time does his flight leave?"

I shrugged. "Four, I think."

"You've still got time." Standing up, she put her hand under my arm and forced me to my feet.

"You mean, go get him, like now?"

"Yeah, why not?"

"Well..." I glanced at the clock on the wall. "I don't know if I can make it in time."

"Yeah, you can." Dad appeared in the doorway behind me. "I'll drive you."

Okay, so that was a surprise.

My lips parted, and I turned to Morgan to make sure I wasn't seeing things. Her grin was delicious. "Just take it." Pushing me toward him, she snatched my purse off the table by the front door and double-checked I had my wallet.

I paused at the bottom of the stairwell.

"Whether you're back this afternoon or in two days, she's going be safe, loved, and cared for, so just go!"

I shot my sister a disbelieving grin as Dad pulled me out the front door.

FORTY

JODY

I was a nervous wreck on the way to the airport. What was I going to do? Fly to New York! No, I'd made my decision, but Leo... Leo wanted New York...and me. And I wanted Leo...and kind of New York, but what about Angel?

My mind felt like scrambled eggs as I tried to figure it all out. All I knew without a doubt was that I wanted Leo, Angel, and me to be a family together, and it almost didn't matter where in the world that happened.

Dad was driving like a maniac trying to get me to LAX. I was grateful for it but struggling to find the words to tell him that. I still couldn't believe he was doing this. I thought he didn't want me whisking his granddaughter across the country where I could neglect her again.

I closed my eyes, feeling sick.

Dad jerked to a stop at the red light, drumming his fingers on the wheel and checking his watch again.

"We'll make it." He nodded.

"That's not it." I shook my head. "I'm just not sure what to do."

"You'll know." The light changed to green and Dad screeched through the intersection.

"Thanks for trying to get me there on time."

"It's the least I can do, Jo-Jo."

I flicked a glance at him. Had I missed something? Was that remorse on his face?

"Why are you helping me?"

He kept his eyes on the road, not glancing my way. His jaw clenched tight, and then he let out a sigh. "This guy, Leo, he makes you happy, and I can tell he really cares about you." Finally his eyes hit mine for a brief second. "I just really want you to be happy, Jo-Jo...and if he makes you happy then..."

He couldn't say it. I could see he wanted to but just couldn't form the words.

He'd give Angel and me up if it meant we were happy.

A rush of emotion coursed through me. "The day Angel fell, why were you calling me?"

Dad's lips pressed together, his right shoulder

hitching. "I was going to try to apologize, figure out a way for us to stop fighting."

A shaky smile formed on my face. "Oh, Dad, I'm sorry I let you down. I'm sorry I've put you through any of this."

He shook his head with a frown. "I was wrong to treat you like I did. I guess I was just so heartbroken that some guy had treated my baby girl, my shining star, with such disregard and then you gave it all up. I was scared. I was scared that you were going to regret keeping Angel."

"Me, too." My voice shook.

"But you're not like your mom. You give people everything, Jody, and you don't hold back. You know how to love with your whole heart. You're not going to turn your back on Angel, you couldn't if you tried. Even after that jackass left you high and dry, there was no bitterness. I carried that for the both of us, and because he wasn't around, I took it all out on you." He glanced my way again, his eyes sad and haunted. "I'm sorry for being so hard on you." His voice hitched and a lump formed in my throat. Tears blurred my vision. "It was just all so unfair, and I got caught up in that, and I missed the fact that you took it and turned it into sunshine, just like you always do." His smile was rich and familiar. Man, I'd missed that smile.

I blinked, letting my tears fall unchecked. "Thanks, Dad."

He reached over and squeezed my knee. "You found Angel the perfect father, and you made a life for yourself...and you did it all without me."

Wiping my finger under my nose, I sniffed and slashed at my tears.

"I'm proud of you, Jo-Jo. I know you'll make the right decision."

"I still don't know what that is, but I really needed to hear all that stuff from you just then." I sucked in a ragged breath and pressed my lips together, trying to contain the child-like sob I wanted to set free.

Dad's thick fingers patted my leg as he blinked at his own tears. "You'll know." He sniffed, pulling himself together before any tears could actually fall. "When you get to the airport and see him, you'll know."

I nibbled at my lip, still not feeling sure.

"No matter what you choose, you have to sacrifice something, but with that loss will come an amazing reward. Morgan's right, don't just think about what you *want*. Think about what you actually *need*. I'm sure there's a song about this." His head tipped to the side and my mouth dropped open.

"You have a song for this moment?"

He looked at me, a sweet little grin pushing at his lips. "Yeah, I heard you guys singing it one time when you were watching *Glee*. Something about not getting what you want, but getting what you need. I think you should keep that in mind."

A quick smile bloomed on my face as the old Rolling Stones song "You Can't Always Get What You Want" shot out of my mouth.

"That's the one." Dad nodded his head, letting

me sing the chorus through. I could tell by the grin on his face that he loved the sound of my voice. As we pulled onto the airport off-ramp, he glanced my way. "I love you, Sunshine."

My heart swelled in my chest, the answer to my big dilemma ringing loud and clear within me.

FORTY-ONE

LEO

The airport was crowded. I didn't know why I expected anything less. I guess I just felt like a little space so I could mope. The niggle within me wouldn't settle. I'd be an idiot to deny the fact I did not want to fly to New York without Jody and Angel.

That plan had made me happy.

The revised version did not.

Glancing to my right with a heavy sigh, I noticed the woman beside me. She was long and willowy with a sharp nose. She had a headphone bud in each ear. I couldn't help wondering what she was listening to. I still hadn't found a song for my melancholy moment, and that was disconcerting, as well. When did I ever *not* have a song?

The guy beside her tapped her shoulder, and she pulled out her earphone to listen to him. I heard the faint music she had playing and scoffed out a dry laugh. "Nothing Without You" by Olly Murs. Kill me now. It was bloody perfect.

Pinching the bridge of my nose, I shuffled in my seat and tried to ignore the words filling my brain. Being a big fan of Olly Murs, I knew the song well, and the lyrics pumped through me, making that hollow feeling in my chest grow with each beat. Each word was another chip of the chisel. I already felt raw and restless; this seriously was not helping.

Snatching up my bag, I flung it over my shoulder and walked to the other side of the waiting area, plonking down in a seat by the window. I stretched out my leg, trying to get comfortable, but I couldn't. My muscles were taut, and I wondered if I'd ever find that smooth, relaxed feeling I cherished when lying next to my foxy lady.

A smile tugged at my lips as I pictured her beside me. I didn't want to walk away from that.

"Then why the bloody hell are you?" I muttered, slumping down in my chair.

Because I wanted to see my music on a stage. Kev was right. I'd come all this way, but what if...what if meeting Jody at the community board all those months ago had been divine intervention?

What if I'd been brought here for something else?

I sat up, liking the feeling that idea sparked inside of me.

What if I was here because I was Jody's match? What if I was the right guy to be Angel's dad?

Shit, I wanted to be Angel's dad. I wanted to see her grow. I wanted to see those pudgy little arms reaching for me when I walked in the door. I wanted to hear her giggles when I danced her around the living room. I wanted to see the sunshine in Jody's smile as she watched us.

I'd miss all that from New York. Screw Skype; that gave me nothing. I needed to *be* there...to experience it in the flesh.

They were my everything dream, so what the hell was I sitting in an airport for?

Because Jody would kill me if I didn't go. She threatened to dump my arse...unless I could somehow charm those foxy pants right off her.

I grinned but still didn't rise from my chair.

Everyone would tell me I was crazy if I didn't take this chance.

The phone in my bag buzzed. I nearly ignored it but after the third ring, unzipped my bag with a sigh and yanked it out.

"Hey, Bobby. How's it going?"

"You on a plane yet?"

"Nah, just, um..."

"Listen, I know you already told me that you weren't interested, but I wanted to call and give you one final chance to say no."

"What are you talking about?"

"That theater in Santa Monica, you know the one that needs doing up? I know I've set up this awesome chance for you in New York, but every time I look at this building, I think of you."

My insides sparked again, the embers igniting with a flame so fierce it took me off-guard. I shuffled in my seat.

"I've got this idiot interested in the space, and I know he's probably going to tear it down and build some shitty little diner or something stupid. Look, his offer is really good, but I'd be willing to slide the thing right off the table if you're interested in taking that old run-down theater and turning it into something Leo Sinclair, you know what I'm saying?"

It was illogical. Turning down an audition in New York, risking the chance of seriously pissing off Jody and possibly losing her...and taking on a theater that could potentially earn me nothing.

Why was I wanting to shout YES?

"Paging..."

I ignored the loudspeaker, running my hands through my hair as I tried to formulate the right answer.

"Bobby, I—"

My reply was cut short when I heard my name...and then a voice I knew by heart. My breath caught in my throat, my lips parting as the people around me looked at each other in confusion.

"Leo, it's Jody. Don't go. I know you have this amazing opportunity waiting for you in New York, but...but I love you and I want to marry you and I want you to be Angel's dad."

My heart lurched in my chest, a slow grin rising over my lips.

"And I know we can do all of that from New York, but I also want it here, because I love my family, too. My heart is in LA, but if you fly to New York, it'll be there, too. It'll be split in half, and I thought that if I let you go and gave you the shot you've been wanting that it would make it better, but it won't, because you'll still be away from me."

The murmurs around me grew as people tried to figure out which waiting passenger the sweet voice was talking to. I sat back in my chair, my eyes transfixed to the ceiling as I waited for more.

"I know that's selfish, because you're so incredibly talented and you deserve every good thing." She sighed, her voice softening to a whisper. "You're my everything dream, Leo. You and Angel, so if we're yours, please stay. Please—"

"Miss, you need to get off that PA system." A stern voice cut her off.

A frown wrinkled my forehead.

"No, please, wait. I need to—"

"Miss! Give me that microphone!"

Nah, no one shouts at my lady that way. I rise from my chair, pausing as I listen to her fight for a little more airtime.

"Please, I have a song for this moment! I just need to—"

"Miss, now!"

"Let me just sing him the so—!"

There was a high screech and then she was

gone. My heart fluttered inside me like a trapped bird. She had a song. She bloody well had a song for me! I wanted to whoop and do a happy dance.

People were chuckling, the murmurs rising in a crescendo around me.

I pressed the phone against my ear. "Bobby, you still there?"

"I am." He laughed. "You still getting on a plane?"

A huge grin engulfed my face. "Not a chance, mate. I've got some sunshine to go kiss."

"Sounds good. Call me tomorrow and we'll talk plans."

"Most definitely."

Shoving the phone in my pocket, I grabbed up my stuff and made a beeline for the exit.

FORTY-TWO

JODY

The security guard looked pissed as he ripped the microphone from my grasp and returned it to the ladies behind the desk. Their cheeks were red as they glanced away from his silent reprimand. I smiled them a sweet thank-you for breaking the rules for me and then turned to the guard. I met his stern glare with narrowed eyes and a little pout. His wrinkles grew deeper with his scowl and he hauled me away.

I had no idea where he was taking me—I was hoping just the exit. A deep sadness washed through me. I didn't get a chance to tell Leo where

I'd be waiting for him. I didn't even know if he'd heard my message.

The phone in my pocket buzzed. I went to grab it, but the security guard wouldn't let me.

"Can I answer my phone, please?"

"Once you're out of this building you can. My job is to make sure you get out that door and don't come back in."

I huffed, jiggling my arm within his beefy grasp.

"Miss, if you resist, things are going to get really bad for you."

"I'm not trying to be a pain in the ass, I just want my boyfriend back."

"There are better ways to go about doing it." His voice was gruff and unimpressed.

He wasn't letting up until I was out those big sliding doors and walking back to Dad's truck. It sucked that I'd failed. I knew I could call Leo in New York and tell him all this again, but I'd really wanted to bring him back home with me from the airport!

The doors loomed large, my heart sinking down to my toes.

"Hey! Hey! Wait!"

I jolted to a stop, gasping at the sound of the Aussie accent hollering behind me. I jerked to turn around, but the guard's grip on my arm only intensified.

"Stop, stop, that's him! He's coming!" I dug my heels into the floor.

With a disgusted snort, the man looked over his shoulder. I strained to glance behind me, and spotted Leo's floppy hair bouncing toward us. My heart rocketed back up my body so fast I felt giddy.

Leo came to a puffing stop beside us, grinning at the guard. "Thanks, mate. I've got it from here."

"I'm not leaving until this girl is out the door."

Patting his shoulder, Leo put on that charming smile of his and tipped his head. "I'm heading out that way. I promise I'll take her with me."

The guard's eyes narrowed.

"Mate, get your hands off my girl." Leo's voice was quiet, yet firm. He still had a smile on his face, but his eyes told the guard he meant business.

With a snort of disgust, the guard let me go and stepped to the side. "If you're not gone in five minutes, I'm arresting you both."

"Fair enough. I'm just going to kiss her and then we're gone."

The guard rolled his eyes and moved away from us. I thought my heart might melt as Leo slid the bag off his shoulder and pulled me into his arms. "C'mere, foxy pants."

I wrapped my arms around his neck, squeezing tight as he lifted me off the ground.

"You didn't go," I whispered.

Popping me back onto my feet, he rested his hand against my face, gliding his thumb along my jawline.

"What kind of moron would get on a plane when the lady he loves basically proposes over a PA system?"

I grinned, my cheeks growing warm.

"Besides, I had to hear this song."

"Oh, yeah." I chuckled, threading my fingers into the hair at the nape of his neck and singing, "Baby Now That I've Found You."

My hips swayed as I sung through the first chorus, Leo's smile growing as he ran his hands down my body, resting them on my hips.

"That's pretty good, foxy, but it's not perfect."

"Oh, no?"

Pulling me toward him, he lifted me into his arms and brushed his nose against mine. "That song says I don't need you, but I do."

I felt like I was going to cry. The look on his face was pure magic. "Even though I'm asking you to give up something you really want?"

"But you're not, Jo, because I want you. You and Angel. I need to be a family with you guys. We can work out everything else around that."

"We're your everything dream, huh?"

He grinned. "You like the alternate ending?"

"Yeah." I nodded, brushing my lips against his. "It's our ending, Leo. It's the dream we're meant to choose."

His smile was divine, his green eyes brilliant as he drank me in. "How 'bout we go start living it then."

"How 'bout you kiss me first," I whispered against his lips.

With a gruff chuckle, Leo obliged, his arms tightening around my waist as his tongue dove into my mouth and claimed what was already his.

I could feel the security guard hovering nearby, but he knew better than to interrupt this kiss. It was epic, perfect...everything Leo and I needed.

EPILOGUE

JODY

One month later...

The little old theater in Santa Monica smelled musty and stale. I imagined it would for a week or so until we really managed to air the thing out. Placing my hands on my hips, I did a slow spin, taking in the cracking leather seat covers and scratched-up armrests. The place looked like the opening scene from *Phantom of the Opera*, on a much smaller scale of course. It had potential, though.

I glanced up at the stage, a grin stretching my cheeks wide as I watched Angel totter across the open space. Cole was waiting on the other side with his arms stretched wide, his smile broad as he clapped his hands.

"C'mere, you little cupcake." He snatched her up when she was within reach, throwing her in the air. She giggled and squealed, dropping a nice big drool on his nose.

"Aw, gross!" He grimaced, wiping the spittle off his face. Ella ruptured with laughter, covering her mouth when he shot her a dry look.

"Good job, Angel." She giggled, jumping up on the stage and wrapping her arm around Cole's back. He pulled her in close and kissed the top of her head.

"You're just lucky I love you so much, Birdy." He tapped her butt with a cheeky grin. She gazed up at him, their eyes both sparkling as their lips met for a kiss.

I watched them with a smile, wondering if that was what Leo and I looked like when we stood as a little family waiting to cross the street or wandering down the pier.

Since Leo had raced through the gates and made all my dreams come true, things had gone from amazing to spectacular. We were back in our apartments in Santa Monica, although this time Leo was living with me. His apartment had been turned into a workspace. We'd moved out all the furniture except the piano and his recording equipment. It was the size of a small studio, which we planned to use for auditions when we were ready to start casting for his musical.

The guy in New York had been disappointed but had to concede that the play belonged to Leo and he could do what he wanted with it...and what he wanted to do was produce and direct it...with me. I wasn't taking the lead; I couldn't spare that much time with raising Angel, as well, but we'd agreed I'd play understudy and also take a small role. We'd also agreed that I'd help with casting, which I was super-excited about. We were planning on using performing arts students from local colleges and high schools. It'd be a great chance for them to hone their skills and, well, it was kind of all we could afford.

First things first, though, we had to get the theater up and running. In order to save a little cash, we'd decided to try to do as much as we could on our own, which was where my family came in damn handy.

"Would you stop complaining! You are capable of getting your hands dirty!" Morgan's voice reached me before I saw her. She burst through the back entrance, Sean shuffling in behind her, looking a little pissed off that the last month of his summer break would be spent cleaning up an old theater.

"Baby, I'm just saying I can't afford to get injured doing any heavy lifting. Travis will kill me if I come back to the set broken. I've got a contract. This body is worth money, and I should be resting up before my heavy filming schedule starts again."

Morgan rolled her eyes. "First-world problems, Sean! You can afford a few splinters and if you're that worried about injuring yourself, I'm sure we can find some toilets for you to clean."

He stopped short, his eyes narrowing. "Sean Jaxon does not clean toilets."

She met his gaze, her face forming her *you did not just say that* expression. "Oh, really? Is that because you're a big-time celebrity, because I've got news for you, buddy." She tapped his chest with her long, pointer finger. "Your poo doesn't come out gold, and you still burp like everybody, so man up and get cleaning or I'm firing our housekeeper."

His jaw worked to the side. "Don't you be giving me attitude, woman."

"Or what, you'll whoop my ass?" Her tongue darted out the side of her mouth, a wicked grin dancing in her eyes. I pressed my lips together, hampering my giggle when Sean growled, wrapping his arms around her and kissing her soundly on the lips.

Oblivious to me as their audience, my sister and her fiancé took their time, Sean's hands lingering down her body as they made up.

I grimaced, turning away and leaving them to it.

Angel was still on the stage, now in Ella's arms. Cole stood back pointing up at the torn stage curtain and discussing logistics with my dad. Oh, yay, he came.

I grinned, waving at him when he glanced over

his shoulder. He did a double-take, rolling his eyes and barking, "Hey! Superstar, get your hands off my daughter's ass!"

A giggle burst out of me, and he gave me a cheeky wink before turning back to Cole. Ella stood on the stage, laughing at Morgan and Sean as they made a red-faced trip down the aisle. Halfway down, he captured her hand, lifting it up so she could twirl beneath him. She did a few perfect pirouettes before she reached the stage, and he lifted her with ease onto the raised platform.

Her head tipped back with a laugh at something he said. He jumped up on the stage beside her, his white teeth gleaming as he pulled her to stand against him. Walking across to Ella, Morgan wrapped my best friend in a hug, kissing Angel's cheek and making my daughter giggle, before doing her typical inspection of Angel's chin. The wound had healed nicely and only a small scar remained.

The picture on the stage made my eyes glisten, I couldn't help it. It was so beautiful.

Angel looked over at me, a smile lighting her face when I waved at her, and then she squealed, pointing behind me. "We-O!"

"G'day, cherry blossom!" I spun in time to see Leo blow her a kiss, which only made my eyes shine even more.

His arm curled around my shoulder, his cheeky smile softening when he noticed my expression. "Hey, what's wrong?"

"Nothing." I shrugged.

His face crinkled with a disbelieving frown.

I laughed, tucking a curl behind my ear. "I'm just so happy."

His smile was gentle, his barely there dimple scoring his cheek.

"I can't believe I'm getting everything I want. It doesn't seem real sometimes. You gave up Broadway for me."

Stepping into my space, he wrapped his arms around me and rubbed his nose against mine. "I didn't give up anything I didn't need."

I brushed my lips over his, my smile growing wide as I started to sing the bridge of "You Make Me Happy" by Lindsey Ray.

He chuckled, his breath warm against me as he took the next line and changed the first word from hope to *know*. It made all the difference. We didn't have to hope anymore. We had that feeling and it wasn't going to end.

I giggled, my hips swaying with the beat as we sang through the rest of the chorus.

Lifting my arm above my head, he spun me around and then caught me against him, cutting my singing short with his soft lips on mine. Pulling off his beanie, I ran my fingers through his hair, feeling that giddy high as he picked me off the ground and reminded me that everything I'd ever need was in this little run-down theater.

#####

Thank you so much for reading *Everything*. If you've enjoyed it and would like to show me some support, please consider leaving a review on the site you purchased this book from.

*****

If you'd like to stay up-to-date with the SONGBIRD SERIES, please sign up for the newsletter, which will include cover reveals, teasers, and new release info for all the Songbird Novels.

http://eepurl.com/1cqdj

HOME is the next Songbird Novel and is due for release in August 2015.
You'll meet two new characters - Josh & Rachel.
I'm so excited to write this story!

You can find the other Songbird Novels on Amazon.

FEVER

Ella & Cole's story

BULLETPROOF

Morgan & Sean's story

.

ACKNOWLEDGEMENTS

It's so cool to get to work with all these amazing people to pull together a project like this.

Thank you so much to:

My critique readers: Cassie, Anna, Theresa, Ashley, Megan, and Brenda. Your enthusiasm over this story was a huge confidence booster. Your feedback was the best!

My editor: Laurie. I love working with you so much.

My proofreaders: Kristin, Lindsey, and Karen. Keep up the great work, girls. What would I do without you?

My cover designer and photographer: Regina. Oh, man, another amazing cover! You are a genius.

My publicity team: Mark My Words Publicity. You make my job a million times better. Thank you so much for all your hard work.

My fellow writers: Inklings and Indie Inked. I check in with you most days, and I wouldn't have it any other way. Thanks for the constant support, advice, and encouragement.

My Fan Club and readers: THANK YOU! I wouldn't be here if it weren't for you guys — xoxo

My family: I love you all so much. Thanks for bringing sunshine into my life and always believing in me.

My savior: Thank you for helping me realize my dreams. I love the life I live, and I credit you for that. I love you.

OTHER BOOKS BY MELISSA PEARL

The Songbird Series

Fever—Bulletproof—Everything

Coming in 2015: Home — True Love

The Fugitive Series

I Know Lucy — Set Me Free

The Masks Series

True Colors — Two-Faced— Snake Eyes — Poker Face

The Time Spirit Trilogy

Golden Blood — Black Blood — Pure Blood

The Betwixt Series

Betwixt — Before — Beyond

The Elements Trilogy

Unknown — Unseen — Unleashed

The Mica & Lexy Series

Forbidden Territory

Forbidden Waters (due for release in May 2015)

Find out more on Melissa Pearl's website:
http://www.melissapearlauthor.com

ABOUT MELISSA PEARL

Melissa Pearl is a kiwi at heart, but currently lives in Suzhou, China with her husband and two sons. She trained as an elementary school teacher, but has always had a passion for writing and finally completed her first manuscript in 2003. She has been writing ever since and the more she learns, the more she loves it.

She writes young adult and new adult fiction in a variety of romance genres - paranormal, fantasy, suspense, and contemporary. Her goal as a writer is to give readers the pleasure of escaping their everyday lives for a while and losing themselves in a journey…one that will make them laugh, cry and swoon.

MELISSA PEARL ONLINE

Website:

melissapearlauthor.com

YouTube Channel:

youtube.com/user/melissapearlauthor

Facebook:

facebook.com/melissapearlauthor

Twitter:

twitter.com/MelissaPearlG

Pinterest:

pinterest.com/melissapearlg/

You can also subscribe to Melissa Pearl's Book Updates Newsletter. You will be the first to know about any book news, new releases and giveaways.

http://eepurl.com/p3g8v